"I wouldn't leave, even if you begged."

Danielle brushed her breasts against Nick's chest, and her lower body teased his erection. "Does that mean you can't take no for an answer?"

Her tone was light, teasing. So like the woman he'd known one hundred years ago, and yet entirely different.

He grinned. "I wouldn't know."

"Hasn't any woman ever told you no?" she asked.

"Not that I recall."

She grabbed his backside and yanked him close, with a hard demand that shot his blood temperature to a dangerous level.

"Well, you won't be hearing it tonight, either, Nicholai Vaux," she said, pronouncing every syllable of his name perfectly, as if she'd spoken the Gypsy name every night for the past century. "Nothing brings us together tonight but us. No magic. No tricks. Just passion. Is that enough for you?"

With a growl, Nicholai grabbed her waist and pulled her up, pausing only to answer her question before he devoured her mouth.

"With you, nothing will ever be enough."

Blaze™

Dear Reader,

Who would have guessed that Danielle Stone would be back so soon? When I first wrote this character in my August 2003 Blaze novel, *Up To No Good*, I never dreamed she'd ask for her own story the minute she finished rehab. Little minx. Kicks her bad habit and bam, she's ready for true love! Not wanting to start a precedent by arguing with such a headstrong woman, I decided to give her a go. Besides, I'd had this charming, sexy Gypsy haunting me since I finished "Surrender," my novella in last month's *Essence of Midnight*. They created a very interesting pair and I hope you'll enjoy reading their story as much as I loved writing it.

Thanks to your letters and e-mails, I know how much you enjoy the continuing characters in my books. If you want to know more about how my stories relate, please log on and visit my Web site at www.julieleto.com. Click on the "Character Connections" link and have fun! While you're there, please take a minute to drop me a note. I love hearing from you!

Happy reading!

Books by Julie Elizabeth Leto

HARLEQUIN BLAZE
4—EXPOSED
29—JUST WATCH ME...
49—DOUBLE THE PLEASURE
92—LOOKING FOR TROUBLE
100—UP TO NO GOOD

HARLEQUIN TEMPTATION
686—SEDUCING SULLIVAN
724—PRIVATE LESSONS
783—GOOD GIRLS DO!
814—PURE CHANCE
835—INSATIABLE
884—WHAT'S YOUR PLEASURE?
920—BRAZEN & BURNING

UNDENIABLE

Julie Elizabeth Leto

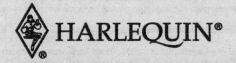

HARLEQUIN®

TORONTO • NEW YORK • LONDON
AMSTERDAM • PARIS • SYDNEY • HAMBURG
STOCKHOLM • ATHENS • TOKYO • MILAN • MADRID
PRAGUE • WARSAW • BUDAPEST • AUCKLAND

For my sisters-in-law
Jeanne, Sharon, Marge, Nicole, Joy, Denise and Jeannette
Your support and love means the world to me.
Here's to always having romance in our lives!

And for Catherine Beredjick, who corrected all my French. *Merci!*

In memory of Charles P. Klapka, Raymond Glatkowski and Orrin Powell, beloved father-in-law and uncles. You are all missed.

RECYCLED PAPER
· RECYCLED PAPER ·

ISBN 0 073 79150 X

UNDENIABLE

Copyright © 2004 by Julie Leto Klapka.

Prologue

"SHE ISN'T SOFIA."

Despite her gentle tone, Alexis's words slashed hot and cruel across Nicholai's chest. Why couldn't his cousin see the obvious? Why did she always have to be so damned certain he was wrong? As always, Alexis's world existed in stark black and white, true or untrue. Real or unreal. Nicholai, since the discovery of the photograph, faced a life growing grayer and less certain by the moment.

He squeezed his eyes shut, but despite his childish, unspoken wish, Alexis and her sweet expression had not disappeared when he opened them again. Back when they were ghosts, he'd often succeeded at wishing her and her calming voice away. Now that they were alive again, he couldn't block out the sympathy in her eyes or the tremor of heartbreak in her voice.

He didn't want her pity. He wanted her help.

"Alexis," he said, reaching toward her.

She shook her head, her hands folded softly over the magazine. "No, Nicholai. You have to accept the truth."

Nicholai cursed, pushing away from the table so hard, his chair slammed to the floor behind him.

"She *is* Sofia! Look at her. *Look.*"

With a shove, he sent the magazine flying across the table. The pages fluttered over the edge and not surprisingly, fell apart on the way down, as the staples surrendered to his abuse. Glossy sheaves of paper skittered across the floor, disconnected and purposeless.

Just like him.

He speared his hand through his hair—one remnant of his former life. He'd changed his clothes, his accent, even his name. But he wouldn't alter everything he had been, especially not a part of him that Sofia had loved so much. His wife had spent hours upon hours tangling her fingers in his hair, seducing him with the soft strokes across his scalp, plaiting the strands into a braid she'd tie with two inches of ribbon cut from her favorite dress. If he surrendered to a haircut of a more modern style, she might not recognize him when the time came.

And the time would come, despite his cousin's doubts.

With her usual quiet acceptance, Alexis bent to the ground and reassembled the magazine. She slid back into her chair, hardly disturbing the atmosphere around her, which crackled with tense silence. She was so gentle, graceful. Quiet. The polar opposite of him—and his beloved wife.

Her sad eyes set her apart from him even further. Nicholai couldn't remember either him or Sofia ever being less than blissfully happy, while his cousin seemed to see the world through a frozen veil of tears.

And he'd yelled at her without provocation.

What a jerk.

His stomach and shoulders clenched with regret.

Maybe Alexis simply couldn't see what was so obvious to him. Yes, she'd known Sofia since childhood just as he had, but maybe the century that had passed had altered her memory, whereas his was fully intact. Was he fortunate or a fool? Either way, he couldn't take what little was left of his family for granted. Unless he made amends, Alexis would torture him with her silence until he burst with guilt. Of all the women he'd ever known, including Sofia, only Alexis was immune to his charm—especially after he'd hurt her feelings.

"Please, Alexis," he said, as he righted the chair. "I have a chance to have Sofia in my life again. Do you really think I should ignore the sign?"

Alexis smoothed her soft hands over the page with the photograph, pressing out the wrinkles. "It's impossible, Nicholai. Sofia died in France over a hundred years ago, three years before we met our fate here in America. And this woman's name is Danielle Stone. She lives in Chicago. How could she possibly be Sofia?"

Nicholai spun the chair around and sat with his arms crossed over the back. "Less than a year ago, you and I had both been dead for over a hundred years as well. Then Viktor's magic brought us back. Is it so hard to believe that Sofia found a similar magic?"

Alexis frowned, her ruby lips curled in a thoughtful pout. "But this woman has a brother. Look here," she insisted, turning the page toward him. "The article is about Sebastian Stone, a—"

She turned the page and read the caption to remember his profession.

Nicholai didn't have to reread anything. He'd already memorized all that the report had revealed. "—venture capitalist," he supplied. "Yes, I know."

Alexis's frown spread to crinkles on her forehead. "I don't even know what that is."

Nicholai grunted. Despite his intense study of the modern world over the past year, there was still so much to learn. "A venture capitalist is a rich man who invests his money in other businesses in hopes of making more money. Sebastian Stone is one of the richest men in the world."

Alexis nodded, but he wasn't sure if she understood or if she simply didn't care about the significance of Stone's wealth. Alexis, like Nicholai, had been raised to eschew wealth and possessions. Gypsies borrowed the earth, they didn't own it.

"If Sofia had been brought back like we were, she wouldn't have had a childhood with this man. She'd have no family at all," Alexis continued, her voice so melodious, Nicholai found himself relaxing despite the tension that had twisted through his body since he'd first found the photograph in the magazine.

Sofia. His Sofia. Alive.

Alexis cleared her throat when his lack of response annoyed her.

"But I have you," he said, singsonging his voice, hoping a more genial tone would win him a reprieve from Alexis's ire. "And Jeta. We're a family. We crossed through the barrier together. We cheated death, Alexis. Don't we owe it to ourselves to grab what life puts before us?"

Her lips twitched, but the frown remained firmly in place. He cursed, but this time under his breath. She was a hard case, his cousin. But with time, he'd break through and convince her they needed each other. He always did.

"We're only here together because we died together," Alexis insisted. "The only person who might have died with Sofia is the man who killed her. But this man," she gestured toward the photograph of Sebastian Stone, a man even Nicholai had to admit he'd never seen before—not in the past or the present, "he's a public figure. If he popped into the living world out of nowhere, don't you think someone would have noticed? If Sofia came back from the dead as we did, she'd have no past. No identity. Definitely no family. That's not the case with this woman. She looks like Sofia, Nicholai, I'll admit that. But she can't *be* her."

Nicholai's frown suddenly matched Alexis's. He'd considered all that Alexis so patiently and logically pointed out. But he'd also contemplated the possibility that a different type of magic had conjured Sofia from the Otherworld. Maybe a magic beyond that of the gypsies.

He'd discussed the possibilities with Evonne Baptiste, the woman who'd taken in his family after their miraculous reentry from their nineteenth-century deaths into twenty-first century lives. Eve, an expert in Romany legend, lore and culture, had for many years been his conduit between the world of the living and the prison of the restless dead. She possessed the power to communicate with spirits who hadn't crossed over and since he and his family had been murdered in a field that was now Eve's backyard, she'd become their contact to the living. No, she'd become more—their friend.

Then just a year ago, she'd discovered an enchanted perfume bottle containing the spirit of a gypsy king who'd been trapped inside. Together, Eve and Viktor Savitch, the imprisoned gypsy king, had created a new magic that had allowed Viktor, Nicholai, Jeta and Alexis to cross back into the living world. None of them were entirely sure how the process worked, but after a year, they'd come to accept the situation as a wonderful gift of fate.

And ever since Nicholai had discovered the photograph in the magazine he'd been reading in order to understand the concept of modern economics, Eve had also shared with him all she knew about another mystic occurrence called reincarnation. Nicholai had become instantly fascinated by the belief that the human spirit seeks perfection by attaining rebirth and that with each new life, issues and problems of the past are faced again. This belief contradicted all he had been taught by his own people. To the gypsies, death was absolute. Yes, spirits often roamed the living world, but usually only to act as guardians and guides—or because they hadn't been properly buried after death. Or, because they'd been murdered—as Nicholai and his family had been.

Yet everything he'd learned from Eve had shown him how limited the knowledge of the old gypsies had been. Maybe Sofia hadn't crossed over from the world of the dead into the world of the living like he had. Perhaps, she'd been reborn.

And if this was the case, and if other beliefs about destiny and karma were true, then his spotting her photograph in the magazine had been no accident, either.

Their spirits were seeking each other in the quest to settle the matters left so unsettled before.

Sofia had died because Nicholai hadn't been there to protect her. How could he spend one more minute in Atlanta, when Sofia—Danielle—was only a few states away?

"I know you don't understand all that Eve told us about reincarnation," Nicholai said, determined to explain. It was the gypsy way to act on behalf of the family, the clan. He would search for Sofia without Alexis's approval, but he wanted his cousin to understand. "It is not what we believe. But the world is a bigger place than it was when we lived, Alexis. Even the Romany are different. The traditions etched into our souls from birth are no longer the same. But my love for Sofia has never dulled, you know that. I need her, Alexis. And I intend to have her."

Alexis's dark hair brushed forward, an undulant black wave against her olive skin, covering eyes Nicholai knew were filled with pity.

He didn't turn his gaze away. He'd rather be pitied than dead. He'd been dead. In many ways, still felt dead, as he had the moment he'd realized that Sofia had disappeared. How they'd searched and searched! In the end, they'd found nothing but her scarf clinging to a branch near a cliff above the ocean, the ground around the edge scuffed, as if there had been a struggle.

Someone had murdered his wife, pushed her over the edge into the churning ocean one hundred yards below. He hadn't been there to protect her. When he'd tried to discover who had killed her, he'd been accused of the crime himself. Without his family, Jeta and

Alexis included, he never would have escaped the gallows. Could he go on this quest without at least their blessing?

He had to. He had another chance at life and he wasn't about to let his cautious cousin derail his intentions. His grandmother had remained strangely, but resolutely, silent about the matter.

"Nicholai, please," Alexis begged, her voice tinged with the Romany accent she and their grandmother, Jeta, had made no effort to erase.

Nicholai, on the other hand, had used this past year to transform himself into a real American. He'd studied speech patterns on television—not the regional news stations in Atlanta, but the national programs where everyone sounded the same. He'd studied magazines and newspapers, adopting the fashion that best suited him—mainly denim jeans, shirts and work boots, since he'd decided the one other thing he'd keep from his past was his trade as a carpenter.

He stood, his palms flat on the table. "Do not plead with me, Alexis, just as I will not beg for your help any longer." He hated the cool tone of his voice, but knew he'd get nowhere arguing with his headstrong cousin. "You believe what you must, and I will, as well. I'm going to Chicago. I will find Danielle Stone. Then I'll know if she's my Sofia."

"Good for you."

The booming voice swung them both around. Viktor Savitch stood in the doorway, looking every inch the gypsy king he'd once been. Proud, strong and resolute. If Viktor had been the head of his clan, Nicholai would have gladly followed him.

"You can't support this folly," Alexis insisted, her eyes narrowed. For some inexplicable reason, Nicholai's cousin hadn't taken much of a liking toward Viktor. They'd come to a quiet truce because Alexis did value her friendship with Eve, who remained Viktor's lover. But at certain moments, like this one, Alexis had no trouble unfurling her claws.

"What has he to lose, Alexis? He only wants to meet the woman, see for himself if any of his Sofia exists in her."

Nicholai crossed his arms, his smile admittedly smug. No need to argue with Alexis when his friend had already shaved the matter down to…what was the popular American phrase—the bottom line?

"He could have his heart broken. All over again."

Viktor's eyes lit up with laughter, but he was smart enough not to so much as grin at Alexis's sentimentality. "Hearts break. They also heal."

Alexis glanced away, piquing Nicholai's curiosity for a moment before he realized he had no time to delve into his cousin's personal life when his was on the brink of triumph or disaster. Alexis would have to work out her demons on her own. When she turned toward him, the fire in her gaze made him wonder if her demon wasn't closer to the surface than he'd ever imagined.

"And just how will you approach her?" She gestured wildly with her hand, her bracelets jangling against the beads that hung from her shawl. Nicholai hadn't seen Alexis this animated in a long time. "Just waltz up and say, *I'm Nicholai Vaux, your husband?*"

He opened his mouth to speak, but then stopped,

realizing he hadn't really thought that far ahead. He shrugged and smiled. In his old life, he'd never had trouble saying something charming and endearing to Sofia, especially once he'd won her heart. Truth be told, the greatest challenge of his life had been the seduction of his wife. And he remembered the game with great fondness. But before that they'd been childhood friends, compatriots of sorts, as much as a Romany boy and girl could have been in their culture and time.

Today was different. Danielle Stone was a stranger to him. He couldn't exactly burst into her life and tell her the story of her death, his death, her rebirth and his resurrection.

No, honesty definitely wasn't an option unless he wanted to send her screaming for the police.

Nicholai needed a plan. And maybe, some help.

His gaze met Viktor's and the gypsy king's grin couldn't have spread any wider. Nicholai had known from the first time they'd met that the two men had a great deal in common.

"Yes, my friend," Viktor verified with a nod. "I do have an idea."

From his pocket, he produced a perfume bottle. Well, not just *any* perfume bottle. *The* perfume bottle. The one whose magic had helped set them all free of death.

Nicholai cocked his head to the side, intrigued. Viktor wasn't one to jerk him around.

"How can that help? I thought the perfume bottle only amplified the supernatural powers of the person who possesses it. I have no powers."

Viktor turned the glass phial in his hand, holding the crystal to the light so that a burst of rainbow colors glittered around them.

"Let's just say I made a few modifications to the magic, Nicholai. Use this correctly, and Danielle Stone will be yours, body and soul."

1

THE PLACE WAS TOO QUIET.

Danielle Stone kicked the door softly with the toe of her boot. The hinges didn't creak or groan or make any other noise that might set her on edge, but the tingle on the back of her neck was too intense to ignore. Something was not right here. She'd never been to Nick's studio before, but a strong instinct born from her years living on the street could not be disregarded.

"Nick?"

She shouted his name from the hall, not stupid enough to go inside. She dug her hands into the pockets of her leather jacket, then changed her mind and crossed her arms instead. She glanced over her shoulder. No one was in the small warehouse lobby nor was anyone visible outside beyond the glass doors. She peeked at the LCD on her cell phone, noting the time. She was two minutes early, but she could sense someone inside. Still, she heard no power tools or hammers banging, though the nose-tickling scent of sawdust teased her nostrils. She leaned into the doorway, couldn't see much but long stretches of free-standing metal shelving, piles and stacks of wood in various sizes, shapes and colors and the occasional work rag or tool.

She spoke into the warehouse again, but kept her body firmly outside. "Nick? It's me, Danielle. I'm here to see the bed."

Finally, she heard his voice from what sounded like the opposite side of the building, somewhere up near the rafters. His deep baritone boomed across the cavernous space.

"I'll be right down."

She didn't immediately walk in, having to wait a full ten seconds before the flutter in her stomach subsided. The man had an irresistible voice, not to mention hypnotic eyes and a delicious smile. She'd tried so hard not to notice his impressive physical attributes when he'd applied as a contractor for the restaurant job, but there was only so much a hot-blooded American girl could do to ward off a good case of lust when a guy had eyes the color of ink and lashes that went on for days. Not to mention a body honed by years of hard labor. At least she'd corralled her natural inclination to flirt outrageously. She had a lot riding on doing this job right.

Unlike her brother, Sebastian Stone, who'd hired her for this gig, Danielle didn't have a degree from Wharton Business School or Harvard. In fact, she'd only recently earned her high school diploma equivalent. Pure nepotism alone had gotten her this chance to supervise the construction of Pillow Talk, a new restaurant that was about to take the sophisticated palates of Chicago by storm—and, at the same time, make her brother proud of her. She'd done quite a bit in that direction already, admittedly. She'd gained her GED, kicked her drug habit to the door and had opened her

heart to the idea of making new friends, even if that
had, so far, been the hardest battle. But thanks to the
loving intervention of her brother and her best friend—
Sebastian's fiancée, Micki—she'd been given another
shot at life, and one incredible chance to prove she
could be as creative, successful and fearless as Sebastian. She couldn't blow this opportunity to shine by
fooling around with some hot guy in worn jeans and a
tool belt.

Dammit.

If not for Bas and Micki, Danielle might never have
crossed paths with Nick Davis in the first place. But
just over a year ago, her brother had ridden to her rescue like the white knights he claimed to despise. She'd
had a drug problem and with Micki's intervention, Bas
had found her the best rehabilitation center in the
world. After getting her through the rigorous program,
encouraging her arts studies and then bringing her back
to the United States with a choice job offer, Sebastian
had not laid down any ground rules in regard to her
personal life. No ultimatums, no conditions, no random
drug tests. He'd only asked her to try and make wise
choices.

Her brother was a generous man, but Danielle understood that business was business. "Bas" Stone
didn't usually dabble in small ventures like the restaurant project, but Micki and Danielle had used their con-
siderable persuasive powers to convince Bas that he
should invest in their pet project.

Danielle and Micki, as well as Micki's twin sister,
Rory, had all at some point worked for the hottest party
planners in Chicago—Divine Events. The cousins who

ran the place—Cecily, Olivia and Gia Divine—had long dreamed of opening their own restaurant and had come up with a truly original concept. When the perfect space had come available, they'd used all the capital from their main business to secure the building. But they hadn't had funds left over to bankroll the restaurant itself.

Bas had stepped in, but with one condition—he wanted Danielle to oversee his interests. He'd explained to Danielle that she would be his envoy, approving all aspects of the restaurant from the construction and design of the furniture to approval of the menu.

At first, Danielle had thought the whole arrangement totally bogus. She didn't know one thing about construction and even less about restaurants, save how to order takeout. The Divine cousins knew more about food and design than she'd ever learn. And she sure as hell didn't want Bas to coddle her and hand her excellent opportunities just because she was his screwup sister who needed a job.

But her brother also wasn't a man to take no for an answer. To convince her to risk all the self-confidence and determination she'd regained during rehab, he'd sweetened the pot.

"You can paint the walls," he'd said.

Danielle distinctly remembered rolling her eyes so hard, she nearly made herself dizzy. "Oh, thanks. I've always wanted to slap a coat of winter-white on twenty-foot concrete slabs. Can I use a roller or do you prefer a spray can?"

He hadn't laughed. Bas had the incredible ability not to find her sarcasm funny.

"That's not what I mean, Danielle. You're a muralist." They'd gone together to the building the Divines had bought, an old dusty department store long out of business by more contemporary shops. His gaze had swept around the large main room then, eyeing the bare walls with bored interest, a look he'd perfected. "You can put your work here, for all of Chicago to see. I've arranged it with the Divines, who have already seen your portfolio and are quite impressed. But you will be given this opportunity only as a reward for overseeing my interests."

The sensation of her teeth biting into her bottom lip jabbed at her even now. Oh, how she'd salivated at the chance to take those huge, blank walls and fill them with color and life. One glance toward the main entrance and she could see a Renaissance boudoir, peopled by a spoiled duchess sucking on ripe cherries, surrounded by her voluptuous maids. Perhaps a lover, a footman, looking on from the window, lust in his eyes. Yes, this would be perfect for Pillow Talk, a restaurant devoted to sensual delights. A perfect project for her, full of stimulating possibilities, the ultimate outlet for her much-ignored libido.

"You don't play fair," she'd said to Bas.

He'd only grinned, stepped forward and knocked her in the chin like the cocky big brother he was. "That's why I'm so rich."

He'd exploited her greatest weakness. Well, actually, her greatest strength.

With one flick of a pen over a very large check,

Danielle had been promoted from receptionist at Divine Events to the coordinator of a major construction project. Yet despite being completely out of her element, Danielle liked the rush of facing the unknown head on. She was, after all, incredibly bossy. And since she'd straightened out, she was resourceful and organized and possessed a hearty supply of common sense. Her lack of business acumen and contacts made her ultimate achievement a bit dicey, but what the hell? Can't win if you don't try. Could be she'd end up a raging success.

With that confidence propelling her yet again, Danielle marched into Nick's warehouse, slipping slightly when her chunky boots met the sawdust blanketing the floor. She regained her balance before landing on her ass, then glanced around desperately, hoping to hell Nick hadn't seen her nearly fall. Women of confidence did not trip over their own feet.

"I've got sodas in the fridge if you're thirsty," Nick called out, his voice dropping from a second-story loft on the other side of the warehouse.

"Thanks, but I'm fine."

She just wanted to see his work and then get the hell out. She liked Nick, from what little she knew of him, but the man definitely unnerved her. More than once during their brief interactions, she'd caught him looking at her as if he knew something she did not. Something important. Something big.

But not as big as this joint. Danielle whistled. This place in Chicago's Pilsen neighborhood was huge, just as large as the space the Divines had bought for Pillow Talk. Shafts of light poured through banks of grimy windows dropping ten feet below the thirty-foot ceiling. Beneath the sawdust, the floors were polished concrete. Rows and rows of metal shelves stood empty along the walls, but in the center of the cavernous room, Nick's work surrounded her in various degrees of completion, from thick planks of wood to a smooth, expertly carved dolphin twisting over a mahogany ocean wave.

She couldn't help but draw the small carving into her palm. The wood was warm and slick, polished to a glossy shine, but with no discernable coating. The lines of the piece were level and perfectly balanced, the weight remarkably light. She'd never seen anything quite so delicate made from wood. So entranced was she by his workmanship that she jumped when he said her name.

She spun around to find him standing just inches behind her. "Nick! You scared me!"

He didn't look the least bit repentant. In fact, he looked nothing short of delicious.

Just like the first day they'd met, Nick wore a pale blue work shirt rolled up to his elbows. He'd tucked the tails into well-worn jeans that hugged his lean hips and trim waist. He'd pulled his dark hair into a ponytail and a tiny emerald of remarkable quality sparkled in his left ear, lending a flash of color to his overall swarthy appeal. Olive skin, black hair, fathomless eyes. The only light in his expression came from the whites around his obsidian irises and the sparkling straight rows of teeth revealed by his mysterious half smile.

"I'm glad you came."

She fought to remove her tongue from where it had

stuck to the top of her mouth. "We had an appointment." Best to get right down to business. "So, are you ready to show me the bed?"

He arched one brow. "What man wouldn't be?"

She sucked in the sides of her mouth so she could bite both cheeks at once. Man, she'd walked right into that one, hadn't she? He was good. Smooth as silk. Sultry as a summer thunderstorm. Just the type of man she should avoid.

She crossed her arms over her chest, deciding to fight fire with sassy fire. "You're quite the charmer, aren't you?"

His grin unfurled completely. "So I've been told."

"Yeah, well, I've found it's best not to believe everything you hear."

With expert skill, he managed to sweep his gaze from the top of her head to the soles of her boots without making her skin crawl. Instead, a gentle warmth flooded through her veins, but the temperature was deceptive. Just one well-placed touch or well-turned phrase and her insides would spark to a hot and steady flame.

Oh, yeah. He was really good.

She swallowed to free her words. "Now, about the bed?"

He swept his hand to the side and without waiting for him to follow, she maneuvered around several tall sets of shelving and a collection of tools that gleamed with unchecked power and potential danger. She smirked, realizing the devices were likely a lot like their owner.

"I thought perhaps one of the Divines might come

along with you today,'' he said, chatting casually as he nudged a can of stain out of her way with his foot.

"The catering and party business they run keeps them incredibly busy. I think they appreciate having my brother at the helm of the restaurant right now. He has a way of injecting people with confidence.''

"I'd be honored to meet him someday.''

Danielle turned and speared him with her gaze, trying to decipher if the sentiment was genuine. She hadn't realized how sought after her brother was until she'd returned to the States, especially after the magazine article in *Entrepreneur* magazine had featured a picture of the two of them together. She'd become a pseudo-celebrity overnight, receiving invitations to political events and lunches at exclusive restaurants. She'd known from the first that the leeches behind the requests were only out to use her to get to Sebastian, but she hadn't expected the same from a carpenter.

"How do you know of Sebastian?''

Nick dusted his hands off on a red rag he'd stuffed in his back pocket. "He's the main investor in the restaurant, isn't he? I'm a businessman myself now, Danielle. I've done my research.''

She hadn't missed his use of the word "now.''

"What were you before?''

"Just a carpenter trying to make a living.''

"Things have changed?'' she asked, burning with curiosity.

He stopped her with his grin. "Things always change. Every minute of the day. You're not the same person you were a year ago, are you? Two years?''

She couldn't contain a burst of laughter. "You have no idea."

In two years she'd morphed from a hopeless, strung-out junkie to a fragile, healing artist to finally, a wide-eyed businesswoman with more than a million dollars to command. Her brother had taken an incredible chance putting her in charge of the project and she had no intention of disappointing him or the cousins who ran Divine Events. Bas Stone likely didn't care if the restaurant failed or succeeded—his investment was a drop in the bucket of his total portfolio—but there was more at stake here than money.

So much more, even beyond the aspirations of her friends, the Divines. For the first time in forever, Danielle had her own goals—dreams that were large and maybe even unattainable. She wanted to be a success. She wanted to make her brother proud. From the moment he'd put her in rehab to the year he'd insisted that she study art in France, Sebastian had put his entire life aside for her. He'd given her space and unconditional love, which her parents had never done, and with just a phone call from her, he'd travel from any spot around the globe to be at her side. And she'd called him more than once. When the cravings had become too intense. When the urge to take off into the night had nearly overwhelmed her. Desperate not to regress back into the seedy world of addiction and despair, Danielle had clung to her brother like a lifeline and he'd never let her down.

But since she'd moved back to the States, she'd made every effort to regain her once precious independence. And so far, she'd done a damned good job. But she had to remain focused. She had time in her life for two things—her job and her art.

Unfortunately, despite her admittedly sordid and violent past, Danielle had never mustered enough hatred toward men in general to erase her interest in them.

Like the interest she could oh-so-easily feel for hunky Nick Davis.

They finally emerged from the stacks of wood and shelving to a space she could see Nick had cleared of any and all debris. The floor gleamed. Tall lamps, the same kind photographers used, provided an umbrella of light around a California king-size bed. Four posts, connected by a canopy, headboard and footboard, surrounded a mattress swimming in blue silk.

At Pillow Talk, the customers would not sit at mission-style tables with stark chairs or even lounge in intimate booths. The Divines wanted to create a new level of comfort and natural sensuality for their groundbreaking restaurant—so at Pillow Talk, the "tables" would be beds.

And not just any beds. Beautiful, hand-carved fourposters with lush drapery and crisp sheets where patrons would lounge like kings and queens, popping gourmet hors d'oeuvres into their mouths. Beds as stunning as the one Nick presented with little flourish. He simply turned, arms crossed and expression smug, allowing his exquisite workmanship to speak for itself.

Only a different vision popped into Danielle's brain, and for a moment, the beauty dispersed.

Seemed like a lifetime ago when she'd been in a warehouse much like this one, coked out and half-unconscious, stripped of her clothes and her dignity, screwing some faceless dick with a video camera. The memory froze her insides as if she'd swallowed a block of ice, but she didn't push it away. She'd learned in rehab that running from the past would not lead her toward a different future. She'd faced who she was. An addicted runaway so desperate for her next hit that she'd sold her body to the highest bidder. And on the streets of Chicago, the price of a cheap whore wasn't exactly exorbitant.

But even if the porno film had had a bigger budget, no one associated with that business would ever have chosen such a thing of beauty as Nick's bed for a prop. She stepped nearer and the moment her hand brushed against the cool fabric, the old memory dropped to the background.

"Go ahead," Nick urged as he crossed to the other side of the bed. "Lie down."

The front of her thighs collided with the firm soft side of the mattress, encased in a shiny, silky comforter unlike any she'd ever seen in a store, or even an exclusive boutique. A lustrous combination of blue swirls—indigo, navy, sapphire and azure—merged together with delicate gold thread, creating a pattern reminiscent of Van Gogh's famous painting, "Starry Night."

"It's beautiful. Stunning."

His mouth quirked into a grin. Coupled with the spark in his eyes, his face presented a challenge even before he spoke. "The fabric is handwoven. Antique."

"Where did you find it?"

He shrugged one shoulder. "I had some help. But you won't get the full effect until you climb onto the bed. Until your body sinks into the softness and your eyes gaze at the sky. Try it, Danielle.''

Just the way he said her name invoked a shiver that stalked across her skin with the same cunning as a cat on soundless paws. God, this had been a colossal mistake. She shouldn't have come here alone. She should have invited Cecily along, or Micki. Hell, she should have brought everyone she knew.

She'd never been completely alone with Nick Davis before. Even their first meeting in her makeshift office at the construction site had been overwhelming and intimate in the oddest way. Here, she felt like she might melt on the spot and he'd done nothing more than invite her to sample the very piece of furniture she'd contracted him to build. But now, like then, the atmosphere seemed to shift, change, alter so that she couldn't quite anchor herself in her new surroundings. The first time they'd met, workmen had bustled ceaselessly around them. A half-dozen cell phones had trilled. Jackhammers and table saws had banged and buzzed as the steady hum of machinery echoed off the bare, stripped walls that would become Pillow Talk.

And yet, she'd felt entirely alone with Nick. As if no one else existed. As if they'd somehow transported to a plane between two worlds, where only they could live and breathe.

Now they were really alone and the lack of air in the wide-open warehouse caused her to grab the nearest bedpost for support.

What was happening?

''You all right?''

She shook her head, denying the obvious. ''I'm fine. It's hot in here.''

He nodded. "The air will kick on in a minute. The sawdust takes some getting used to."

She inhaled, then exhaled, repeating the process until she felt steady again. Had she not eaten breakfast? Drank too much coffee? Or maybe this was a simple case of sensory overload.

Nick stepped closer, and patted the thick comforter. She'd half expected him to stroke the silk covering, maybe slip onto the bed and beckon her as he reclined, like a sultan commanding the obeisance of a concubine. Instead, he hooked his thumbs in the pockets of his dusty jeans and lifted one eyebrow over bemused, dark eyes.

"Seems you've got a perfect place to lie down until the dizziness passes. Why so reluctant? It's just a glorified dining room table, right?"

Danielle attempted to swallow, but her mouth lacked the moisture to finish the job. How did he do that? How did he bring the most amazingly sensual ideas to her mind when all he was really doing was inviting her to see his work in the same manner that customers would in just a few weeks?

"Of course. I just didn't want to ruin the presentation. The beds at the restaurant won't have comforters as luxurious as this. I believe Gia picked thick sheets in a high thread count. Soft, but functional. I mean, people will be having dinner on them."

She was babbling. She couldn't believe she was babbling. She didn't dare look at him, knowing she'd see laughter in his eyes.

Instead, she shut up and did as he'd invited, sliding onto the bed. The mahogany frame didn't make a sound, not that she weighed nearly as much as a party of four. She ignored the rich softness underneath her and instead turned to look up at the canopy.

She gasped.

He joined her on the bed—a safe foot or two away, but his weight and warmth seemed to travel across the comforter like wildfire on dry grass.

"Is it what you imagined? It's hard to picture here in the workshop, but in the dim lights of the restaurant…"

His voice trailed off and Danielle didn't need him to fill in the blanks. Obviously, he'd studied the design plans of the restaurant more closely than she'd anticipated. Though the ceiling of Pillow Talk was over twenty-five feet high, the space was already implanted with tiny, laser optic lights that could be programmed for any number of configurations. They could change colors for the holidays—red for Valentine's Day, green for St. Patrick's, orange at Halloween. They could simulate fireworks on New Year's Eve and the Fourth of July. But on most nights the Divines planned to create the illusion of a sparkling night sky with glittering white lights on a field of midnight blue.

To complement the view, Nick had carved the canopy to resemble tree branches, leaves and even moss. She couldn't help but climb onto her knees and reach up, so she could run her hands over the polished wood.

"You stained the leaves."

"Just a bit," he said, rolling closer.

She was suddenly aware how her blouse had lifted as she reached, and how his gaze had drifted toward her exposed skin. Awareness danced over her flesh like deft fingers, and yet she couldn't surrender to the rhythm. It was all in her imagination, right? Her very active, sexually deprived imagination.

She refused to move just because of a phantom tingle. Instead, she reached even higher, concentrating on his work, truly amazed at the smooth edges and attention to detail.

He cleared his throat before he continued to speak, but Danielle heard the raspy depth in his voice anyway. The sound of desire was hard to miss, especially when every fiber in her being desperately wanted to hear it.

"The restaurant will be dark, so I added a touch of color that will hopefully pick up the light from the bedside lamps."

With concentration, she turned all her attention to the artistry of his work. He understood the importance of visual presentation, the crucial aspect that lighting played on how an object appeared. Like her, he was an artist. But this was all they had in common. All they'd likely ever have in common.

"Nick, this is amazing."

He didn't respond, but his stare remained a powerful presence below her, boring into her with an intensity that stole her breath nearly as effectively as his craftsmanship. She'd come here to see his work. She'd accomplished that goal. There was no other reason for her to stay.

Stay.

Her gaze darted to his face. His lips hadn't moved.

"Excuse me?"

"What?"

"Did you just say something?"

He tilted his head to the side. "No, but I should have said thank you. It's nice to work with someone who appreciates the details."

She sat back down on the bed, her backside balanced on her heels. "What, you can throw your voice, too?"

His face remained a perfect picture of confusion. "Danielle, what are you talking about?"

Okay, she was losing her mind.

"Nothing. I can't believe I'm the first person to notice your attention to detail."

His grin was a wry quirk. "You have no idea how blind most people can be, especially about things of beauty."

Danielle swallowed thickly. Nick Davis was not a subtle man. The way his words struck her, she imagined he sharpened the points of his flirtations before they left his mouth, then aimed with perfect accuracy so they pierced every barrier she'd erected to keep her heart safe.

"I do know about beauty," she said, deciding right then that the only way to keep from falling victim to Nick's appeal was to concentrate on business. "And this bed is perfect. I want fifteen more just like it."

He didn't flinch. They'd already agreed to the number in the initial proposal—before Danielle had any idea he'd work with such artistry. But according to their phone conversation earlier, he'd already completed the bulk of the work. Now, he was only adding the artistic touches.

Still, he frowned. "They won't all be exactly the same, I'm afraid. I'm a carpenter, not an assembly line. I intended this one to be the centerpiece."

She tore her gaze away from the dreamy look in his eyes and climbed off the bed. She stumbled in her haste, but recovered with a modicum of grace and balance. "Fine. You obviously know what you're doing."

She straightened her clothes and pulled her cell phone from her pocket. Time to get the hell out of here. She called the taxi dispatcher and gave the address. With any luck, she'd have no more reason to confer with Nick for at least a few more weeks.

"Should I have this one delivered tomorrow?" he asked. "For your meeting?"

Damn. Damn, damn, damn. The Divines were assembling at the site tomorrow to assess the project's progress. Having the bed there as a centerpiece would be the icing on the cake.

"Yes. That would be perfect. You think of everything, don't you?"

She had to get out of here quick. She spun toward the door, but had only marched a few feet before he slid off the bed and stopped her.

"I have something for you."

"Oh?"

He disappeared behind a shelf, then reappeared with a wooden box. The minute he placed the small polished case into her hands, she knew it was old. Very, very old.

"What is this?"

"A gift."

She stepped back. "For what?"

"Just a show of appreciation for the contract you awarded me. This is standard business procedure, isn't it?"

She shrugged, unsure. She hadn't been a business-woman long enough to know one way or another. He already had the lucrative contract, so he wasn't exactly buying any favors from her. Still, this wasn't exactly a pen set or a box of chocolates. A warmth thrummed within her as she cradled the box. Just what was inside?

She balanced the box on her upper arms and poised her finger on the latch.

"No," he said.

He'd reached toward her, but drew back his hand before they touched.

"Can't I open it?" she asked.

"Of course. It's just that the object inside is very delicate. You don't want to drop the case. Why don't you just open it after you go home?"

She supposed she should have heard alarm bells warning her about his odd request, but Danielle had known too many truly dangerous men in her lifetime ever to consider Nick one of them. In fact, his gaze dropped a bit, indicating that maybe he was simply uncomfortable with her opening the gift in front of him.

"Fine, whatever you prefer. I appreciate the gesture. You do beautiful work, Nick. I can't be more pleased with your progress."

With that, she turned and left. She marched through the warehouse without hesitating, certain she could feel his gaze on her back, even when she was clearly out of sight.

2

"SHE ISN'T SUSPICIOUS?"

"Of course not," Nicholai said, sliding the crockery pot Jeta had brought him into the preheated oven in his small kitchen. Cooking for himself was one of the few aspects of modern life that he hadn't quite mastered yet. Not that he needed to, as long as his grandmother still lived down the street. "Men give women gifts all the time."

Jeta chuckled, her wizened voice full of conspiratorial joy as she placed fresh fruit into a bowl on his wobbly table. "Don't fool yourself, Nicholai. You've put the wheels in motion, now. There is no turning back."

"I don't wish to turn back, Jeta. I know she is my Sofia. I know. And I'll have her again, just as fate has determined."

Jeta waved her hand, dismissing his use of words and concepts she didn't care to understand. She'd come with him to Chicago for one reason and one reason only—to control the magic.

Jeta had been the wife of a gypsy shaman, and a respected *chovihana* herself. She knew all too well how spells and charms worked, and how they did not. And though Jeta had become friendly with Viktor Savitch,

Nicholai was out of practice in the magical arts. Jeta couldn't trust that the enchanted bottle would work as Viktor intended, as Nicholai needed it to. So she'd decided to travel north with her grandson and keep a watchful eye on how things progressed. Nicholai suspected, however, that Jeta also had ached for the chance to travel. Despite her age, her nature required her to wander. She'd explored the towns and enclaves between Georgia and Illinois. She'd reveled in the diverse cultures of the American South and the Midwest. And she'd adapted perfectly to this city, where ethnic groups clashed or mingled only a few feet from her window.

"Nothing happens by accident," Jeta reminded him. "We've learned this the hard way, haven't we?"

Nicholai remained silent. Too many accidents had marred his previous life. In this one, he would take every turn of fate and work it to his own advantage. Especially where his wife was concerned.

"Did she recognize the bed?" Jeta asked.

He shook his head, unwilling to voice his disappointment out loud. He shouldn't have gotten his hopes up. What were the chances that Sofia—Danielle—would remember a life she'd lived one hundred years ago simply because of a comforter with a pattern like the one Jeta had woven for them as a gift for their marriage? The moment they'd met in her office those weeks ago, Nicholai had recognized the similarities between Danielle and Sofia, beyond the fact that they were physically identical. Like Sofia, Danielle possessed a wariness, a mistrust, that kept strangers at arm's length. But she also trusted her instincts, relied on them. Like him,

Sofia had never possessed any real magic, but she appeared to be powerful simply through her ability to read people for what they truly were.

The one time she'd been wrong, she'd been murdered.

Nicholai shook the memory away. The murder had been over a century before. He had a new life now, and soon, Sofia would have her second chance as well.

"No matter," Jeta decided. "Now that she has the gift, you will have more power over her. The suggestions you feed to her will be stronger. If she is truly your Sofia, you'll know soon."

Nicholai's gut clenched. Did he really want to manipulate her with magic? When Viktor had made the offer, Nicholai had been so sure, so single-minded in retrieving the woman he'd lost so many years ago. But Nicholai had never felt comfortable with what he couldn't see. Growing up with Jeta and Alexis, he'd accepted the reality of forces beyond his understanding like magic and curses and spells. As the wife of the clan's healer, Jeta had been a powerful and feared woman even though she'd never used her magic for anything but tending the sick and every so often, a little tomfoolery. His cousin, Alexis, with her ability to see beyond the physical world, often into the future or the past, had entertained the *gaujo* on both sides of the ocean. Her talent had paid well and kept food in their mouths and a roof over their heads. Nicholai had accepted that sometimes, magic was necessary. And to reclaim his Sofia, he'd do whatever he had to.

"I should have let her open the box here," he said, wondering what Danielle had thought about his strange behavior. He'd half expected her to toss the gift into the nearest trash can on the way out the door. But he'd watched her retreat to her taxi with the box still in her hand.

Jeta clucked her tongue at his doubts. "Viktor said the spell would be more powerful if she opened the box in her home, amid the things she owns and loves. Of course, she might be too curious and open it out on the street. No telling what havoc that might cause!"

Jeta laughed, completely amused as she gathered up the groceries she'd bought at the corner store. Nick had been grateful that his grandmother had supported his quest to move to Chicago and find his Sofia, but her insistence on accompanying him had been a mixed blessing. He'd used his first year of new life in Atlanta learning about the world in the twenty-first century. He'd been determined to acclimate completely and so far, he'd done a credible job. In today's culture, a man who depended on his elderly grandmother wasn't considered a man.

Good thing he was a gypsy, because, otherwise, he'd miss her delicious cooking.

"How's the air conditioner in your apartment?" he asked, helping her toward the door.

"Necessary. All these buildings exhale too much heat."

"I'll walk you."

She snorted. "I'm old, Nicholai, not feeble."

"This is a dangerous neighborhood."

That made her laugh until she nearly dropped her bag. "Nicholai! I've faced bandits more bloodthirsty than the hoodlums outside. They're afraid of me and give me a wide berth."

"And so they should," Nicholai agreed. His grandmother was nothing short of formidable and though they'd been in the city for weeks, she'd yet to run into any kind of trouble she couldn't handle.

"Still, I don't know how much longer I'll be able to stay in this city, Nicholai. This has been a fine adventure, but the concrete chokes me. I miss Evonne's garden."

"I'll send you back now," Nick insisted, walking her out to the street. The sun hadn't quite dropped beyond the buildings, but the sky had turned from blue to lavender. "I can do this on my own, Jeta. I told you before."

She patted his cheek, then waved her hand dismissively. "Yes, of course you can. But it will take you longer and it is not our way to abandon our own to the world of the *gaujo*. Viktor said the magic is temporary once it is unleashed. I may be out of practice, but I'm certain I can give it a little push now and again."

She chuckled as she left, clearly amused with whatever she intended to do to amplify the magic Viktor had lent him. Determined to get what he wanted, Nicholai didn't give the old woman's schemes another thought. As long as he had his Sofia, he'd do whatever was necessary.

"QUELQUE CHOSE NE VA PAS."
   Something is wrong.
   "Non, j'avais juste besoin d'entendre ta voix."
   No, I just needed to hear your voice.

Danielle had no idea why she'd called Armand. They spoke regularly, but she tried never to call him in a crisis. It was too weak a gesture, especially with a former lover. But their relationship defied explanation sometimes. They'd been intimate lovers, and yet, a year after her return from France to the United States, they remained intimate friends. The kind that shared secrets. More than likely, if they still lived on the same continent, they'd occasionally share the same bed.

"Encore les rêves?" he asked.

The dreams again?

"Pas exactement."

Not exactly.

The nightmares he asked about hadn't plagued her for weeks. She still faced nights of disturbing dreams, but they no longer seemed to center around the drug-fogged memories of her life on the streets. Hard concrete. Bitter cold. Debilitating hunger. Slobbering men fumbling for a pound of her flesh. Lately, the monsters in her sleep more often took the form of ill-prepared workmen and unskilled plumbers than heroin-hazed junkies willing to share their stash in exchange for a quick blowjob.

"Then what?" he asked, his heavily accented English spiking her blood pressure. What was it about men with accents?

"Work."

He groaned and Danielle forced a laugh. How often had she wasted overseas long-distance phone time griping to her former lover about the pressure of her new job? The stubbornness of some of her contractors? The loneliness that often drew her back to the streets she once haunted as a doped-out, screwed-up runaway? Did this make her weak, allowing Armand to remain her anchor, her ultimate listener, her teacher? She smiled wryly, remembering how she'd balked when Sebastian had enrolled her in a prestigious art school in Paris immediately after her release from rehab. Her brother had encouraged her to hone her skills as an artist before she returned to the United States. He'd wanted her to enjoy a free-spirited lifestyle completely opposite from the one she'd experienced on the mean streets of Chicago.

Back then, she'd had trouble believing her art had merit. At that point, all she'd known was that during the hours she spent layering in the details of an extensive mural, her mind cleared. She stopped focusing only on herself, on her needs and disappointments, and suddenly had a vision of a world outside her own. When she painted, her cynicism and anger melted away like the chocolate coating poured over virgin-white ice cream on a sultry summer day.

Then she'd met Armand. He'd taken her natural pessimistic attitude and shaped it into the edge she'd needed to become a truly talented artist. He'd been her mentor at first, then soon after, her lover. Now, he was her friend. The memories of their affair often kept her sane on the nights when the shadows of her past threatened to strangle her with regret and fear.

"Work disturbs you, but that is not what I hear in your voice, *mon amour*. Is it the cravings? Are they back?"

Danielle cleared her throat. Yes, they were…but not the ones Armand expected. She was working in the restaurant industry now, where alcohol flowed and drugs from speed to Ecstasy were readily available. Who was she kidding? Drugs were readily available to anyone who knew how to find them in any industry. Especially when you knew the scene from the inside out.

But it wasn't vice that had her tempted tonight to the point of desperation. No, it was Nick Davis and his sexy voice and sexier body. Not to mention his intriguing gift, which she still hadn't opened.

"What does it mean when a man you barely know gives you a very expensive present?" she asked.

Armand laughed, his voice traveling over the transcontinental link with throaty warmth. "A man is vying for your attention and you don't know what to do? Impossible!"

"This isn't the right time for me to be involved with anyone."

"When is the right time? Look at us. You were fresh out of rehabilitation. *Vulnérable et effrayée.* But I wouldn't let you surrender to your fears or vulnerabilities, would I? And now look at what we have because of it? *Tu es mon âme soeur.*"

Soul mates? She'd once agreed with Armand about that. Did she still?

His voice deepened with his concern. "You don't regret our affair, do you?"

"Oh, God, Armand. Never."

The desperate sincerity in her voice was not exaggerated. She could never repay Armand for the utter joy he'd brought into her life, into her soul. That they'd ended up incompatible on other levels would forever remain a disappointment for her, but Danielle had promised Armand she wouldn't spend one moment regretting their breakup since they'd somehow said goodbye, yet remained good friends. He had taught her so much more than techniques of commanding light and shadow, of broadening her strokes or tempering her vision. He'd taught her that sex wasn't dirty or cheap to be used as barter for anything less than heaven itself.

In his gentle romanticism, he'd helped erase her negative associations with sex. He'd shown her the pleasures the body demanded when the heart and mind were fully engaged.

But until this moment, until the interlude with Nick at his workshop, she'd never considered the possibility of finding intimacy with someone else so soon.

"Why does it bother you that this man gave you a gift?" Armand asked.

"He…unnerves me."

"Lust, it does this."

"It's not lust," she insisted, knowing she was lying through her teeth.

Luckily, she could count on Armand to know that as well.

"If you are living a life without passion, Danielle, you might as well hide away in a cave. Admit it. You are truly living, for the first time in years. You have a job you love to complain about, which to me means you care about your work. You have family that loves you. And I know you paint every night because I hear the joy in your voice. So, finally, a man has found a way to intrigue you amid all the changes you've gone through. What is so terrible?"

"He works for me," she said.

Armand snorted. "The concept of not sleeping with an employee is disgustingly American."

She rolled her eyes. Armand refrained from insulting her country on all political and social matters, but when it came to sex, he was utterly ruthless.

"That's not really the reason he scares me, really. I'm making excuses."

"You said it, not I. Tell me about him."

Danielle settled onto the sofa, not realizing until now that she'd been standing tensely since she'd first dialed Armand's number. She'd called at eight o'clock Chicago time, which made it three o'clock in the morning in France. She'd figured she'd find him either painting or in bed, though she was betting on painting since there was no background noise—no female heavy breathing or cooing or, the worst, giggling. Armand was a wonderful, confident man, but he hated to sleep alone. Unlike Danielle, he'd likely taken another lover before she'd even arrived at the airport to return to the United States. But for some reason, she wasn't jealous. Probably because as much as she loved Armand, she hadn't fallen in love with him.

"This is weird," she muttered, eyeing the box from Nick that she'd placed in the center of her coffee table, but still hadn't opened.

"Why? Do you think I will be jealous?" Armand teased. "I will, you know. I'll always be jealous of any man you take into your bed. I hope you don't mind."

"I didn't say I was going to sleep with him."

He cursed, first in French, then in English for good measure. "Then why are we having this conversation?

I'll hang up now and go back to work. Much more interesting than listening to false claims from a woman I know as well as I know myself.''

''No,'' she shouted, knowing he was teasing, but not so certain he wouldn't hang up just to teach her a lesson. She needed to talk this through with him. If she didn't sort out the conflicting emotions soon, she'd instead find excuses to be around Nick, to get to know him, to explore the electric currents that had sizzled between them from the first. ''I guess I shouldn't make that decision so soon.''

''No, you shouldn't. What does he look like?''

Danielle's eyelids drifted closed, possibly of their own volition, but more likely as a direct result of the overwhelmingly clear picture she could instantly form of Nick in her mind.

''He's a pirate.''

That caused Armand to pause. ''A real pirate? A thief?''

Was that actually envy she heard in his voice?

''If he wore a poet shirt and thigh-high boots, I'd let him ravage me in a heartbeat.''

Armand laughed. ''Ah, then we are talking types.''

Dashing and forbidden. Surrounded by an aura of sensuality. Undeniably sexy.

''Dark hair, of course?'' Armand asked.

''Like midnight.''

''Darker than mine?''

Definitely jealousy.

She bit her tongue. ''Blue-black,'' she answered, snagging her bottom lip in guilty pleasure, not because Armand's possessiveness made her feel good, but because her entire body tingled as she remembered how she'd wanted so desperately to run her fingers through Nick's hair.

"And his eyes?"

Shadows. Dark and unyielding in their mystery, yet quick to sparkle when something amused him. Even quicker to fill with desire, though the blackness hid the secret well.

"Like ink."

"Sounds intriguing. Tell me more."

"Why?"

"Get it out of your system, *ma petite*. If you tell me everything about him, he won't be such a puzzle to you. That's why you're afraid. You don't know him."

"I have a feeling he'd be a puzzle even if I'd known him for one hundred years."

"Un homme mystère? Très érotique."

"You don't know the half of it."

"Tell me."

Danielle tucked the phone between her shoulder and her cheek, then bent down, unlaced and removed her boots. She stretched her toes and ankles, groaning when the tired joints cracked. She unzipped and hopped out of her jeans, suddenly desperate to be free of her work clothes, which likely smelled of sawdust and city grime.

"He has a very powerful aura," she explained. "In Hollywood they'd call it a 'presence.'"

"So he's full of himself?"

"No, not at all. He's quiet, chooses his words. He's charming, but not because of what he says. More like, what he doesn't say."

"What doesn't he say that you want to hear?"

Danielle inhaled deeply. "I think it would be dangerous to know what was going on behind those black irises. God, you should see his lashes, Armand. They're so dark, especially the ones beneath his eyes. It's like he's wearing smudged liner."

"Maybe he is."

The possibility made her erupt with laughter. "He's a carpenter, Armand. He wouldn't be caught dead in makeup."

"What about his hands? Are they rough or smooth?"

Damn. She wished she knew. Probably a combination of both. He had to have calluses, working with heavy wood as he did. But she imagined his fingers must be deft and gentle if they could carve mahogany into tendrils of moss so fine they looked as if a breeze would set them swaying.

"I don't know about his hands. We've never touched."

"Not even when he gave you the gift?"

She shook her head, her gaze drawn back to the carved box on the coffee table. All the way home, she'd wondered if he'd done the carvings on the casket, but the wood and the hinges appeared old. Very old.

"No. As a matter of fact, I think he wanted to touch me, but he stopped."

"Ah," Armand said, knowingly. "He didn't trust himself."

She plopped onto the couch, her bare legs tucked beneath her. She undid the tiny straps holding her blouse together, then snuggled beneath the throw blanket in her panties and bra.

"How do you know that?"

"Because when I was with you, I never trusted myself either."

3

"DIDN'T TRUST YOURSELF, HOW?"

The topic intrigued her. She was fairly certain she and Armand had discussed every topic under the sun until they had nothing more to reveal, nothing more to debate. How could a man as comfortable in his own skin as Armand Rousseau ever not trust himself to touch her? Never once had she believed that her former lover was anything less than an expert in all things sexual and sensual, and that he didn't have a capacity for reluctance in any shape or form.

"You're a very beautiful woman," he said, his answer entirely too simplistic in her opinion.

"So are a lot of women. Most of the women you seduce fall under that umbrella. Why wouldn't Nick trust himself to touch me, especially just on the hand?"

Armand cleared his throat, but his voice still sounded deeper than usual. "Because the lust between the two of you is so strong, one touch might not be enough. Every man has his limits."

Surprisingly, she had no trouble accepting that possibility, likely because she felt the same way.

The connection between her and Nick had, from the first time he walked into her office, been incredibly intense. He'd looked at her with eyes that seemed to have seen her a thousand times before, and yet, with each time, their attraction was reborn and renewed. Like lovers reuniting after a long separation. She'd been so wrapped up in her new job that she hadn't allowed herself to act on the strange sensations, but now, with the work on the restaurant well under way and the frenzy of the grand opening a good six weeks off, Danielle was at liberty to ponder the possibilities. She had no choice with Nick's mysterious gift practically staring her in the face.

"Well, I suppose I should open his present."

She heard the rustle of tarp on the other side of the phone line. "Do you want me to call back? Perhaps it is too intimate. Perhaps you should call this man instead of me, thank him just as intimately."

Danielle scoffed at Armand's suggestion. She doubted Nick would give her anything embarrassing or personal. He wouldn't cross that line, not when she still had his paycheck in her control. Besides, she knew damned well that no matter how much she might be in the mood for a little phone sex right now, she certainly wasn't going to call Nick. Although, just the thought of his unforgettable voice caressing her over the telephone lines, asking her confidential questions, describing his sexual fantasies to her, evoked a pearl of moisture between her thighs. How delicious would a true forbidden encounter be?

Would a man like Nick do such a thing? Did he skate on the edge of taboo? If she'd had the courage to offer him an indecent proposal, how would he react? The possibility coursed through her veins like an electric current. She imagined his eyes, so like a storm, darkening to torrential blackness, just before he accepted her offer and then introduced her to carnal pleasures she'd never experienced, never even imagined.

She balanced the phone between her cheek and shoulder again and popped the tiny gold latch on the front of the box. She scooted forward on the couch, her bare legs suddenly prickling with a cool breeze from the air conditioner. Shifting in her seat, her panties caught a wisp of the draft and chilled the wetness, enhancing the thrill already shooting through her veins.

"I'd rather talk to you," she said, lifting the top gently. "You're safer."

"Insult me, why don't you?"

The hinges resisted, but made no sounds of protest. Her breath caught as the light from the solitary lamp beside her slid over an antique perfume bottle, nestled in scarlet silk, unlike anything she'd ever seen.

Had Armand spoken? Had it been his voice she heard? So entranced by the glittering cut crystal and intricately woven silver in the obviously ancient glass, Danielle couldn't be sure. And she didn't care. Her hands gravitated toward the bottle, her palms aching to feel the beautiful artifact in her hands.

"Oh, my."

She pressed the orange button on her handset, switching the phone to speaker mode, then set it on the couch beside her. She held her breath until the moment she finally cradled the bottle in her palm. A sizzle of warmth snaked through her fingers, around her wrists and up her arms. But the sensation didn't make her want to drop the bottle—just the opposite. She held it tighter, cupping it between both hands.

Danielle tried to come up with words to describe the beauty, but she was at a loss. "It's not like anything I've ever seen, ever touched."

She lifted the bottle to her nose and removed the top. A sudden wave of dizziness struck her, not because of the scent—there was none—but likely because she forgot to breathe. She turned toward the lamp, gasping when the crystal facets seized the light and threw a rainbow of colors over her skin.

"Describe it to me," Armand requested.

His voice sounded so strange through the speaker-phone, so she leaned closer, to make sure he could hear.

"It's a perfume bottle, but it must be a hundred years old, maybe more."

She turned the crystal, carefully examining it from all angles and sides, softly cradling the delicate beauty. Why had Nick given her a gift so precious, so obviously expensive? So clearly enhanced by a life all its own?

Want him.

The voice was clear, crisp, female, but the sound had come from someplace in her head. She knew her own voice, and this wasn't it. Like the disembodied sound she'd heard at Nick's workshop, the voice echoed with a command she didn't dare obey.

Quickly, she put the bottle back in the box and scooted it to the center of the table. She climbed completely onto the couch, practically scrambling into the corner farthest away from the strange gift.

"Danielle?"

Distance didn't help. In one overwhelming wave, her body nearly drowned in a sudden current of desire. Moisture disappeared from her mouth as blood rushed to every separate zone of her body. Her fingers tingled. Her nipples chafed against the lace of her bra. Every sexual impulse, every blast of lust she'd contained since her return to the States assaulted her. Images and memories flew through her mind, but with such speed that she couldn't identify a single one.

What was happening?

"Armand?" she said, pleading.

"Are you all right?"

"I don't know."

"Are you in pain?"

"No. Not exactly. It's…"

She struggled to find words to describe the feeling, but she couldn't meld the sensations into anything solid. She inhaled, exhaled, then repeated the process. She'd learned the technique in rehab, a simple breathing exercise to help her when her cravings threatened to push her over the edge. But this wasn't an insatiable desire for drugs. This was about sex. Hot, sweaty, lusty sex.

That in itself confused her. Danielle had never craved sex, not even when involved with Armand. Yeah, she'd had sex plenty of times before she'd met him, back when she'd been drugged out. But the two activities, sex and drugs, had never truly competed for priority. For Danielle, the drugs had always come first.

Even after she'd cleaned up her act and had taken up with Armand, he had always been the aggressor, the seducer. She responded, but never initiated. Though she'd let go of her negative associations with sex, desire had never entered the picture until Armand had coaxed her sensual instincts to the surface.

With him, sex soothed and healed. Often, it simply passed the time—but always with delight and anticipation. Never with the overwhelming, maddening, physically paralyzing need she was experiencing now.

"Armand, talk to me," she said, certain the rush would pass if she simply changed the subject.

"He wants you."

"I don't want to talk about that."

"I don't remember giving you a choice of topics. He gave you a gift that obviously has excited you, more than it should. What does it feel like?"

To no other man could she admit this. "Like a thousand hot fingertips running over my body. It's not natural."

"We're talking about your body. Of course it's natural. What is it doing to you, those thousand hot fingertips?"

"Making me insane."

"Why? Are they touching you where you want them to?"

No! She realized then that the sensation was not centered on her breasts or between her legs and that when she tried to identify where she felt the invisible hands, the response faded. Was she crazy? She looked at her hands. Had he placed some psychedelic drug on the box, on the bottle itself?

She knew hallucinogens firsthand. This wasn't the same feeling. Despite the quick flash of memories, her brain was clear. Only her body seemed to have a mind and will of its own.

"Run your hand along your neck, behind your hair. Are you hot?"

She did as he requested. They'd done this before, exploring sexual fantasies over the phone lines, but never had the virtual lovemaking centered around the effects another man had on her. But Danielle didn't second-guess the situation. She trusted Armand, and maybe working off some sexual energy would dull the odd effects she was experiencing.

"I'm sweating," she admitted.

"Just from thinking about his hands on you?"

She sighed, knowing there was so much more to it. In an instant, she conjured a decadent picture of Nick here, in her apartment. Undressed. Fully nude and hard and oh-so-irresistible.

"His hands, his eyes, his mouth," she said. "All of the above."

"Where would he touch you first?"

She moaned in anticipation as she considered the question. Nick was a man of intense control, that much she could tell from their brief interactions. The way he'd pulled his hand back when his touch could have been accidental thrilled her to the core. But there was also a deep-seated passion inside him, a ravenous appreciation for life and beauty that shined in his eyes like polished black pearls. His lusty nature likely engaged in a daily battle with his carefully maintained control—and this was a war she knew all too well.

"He'd touch my hand, I think."

"He's shy."

"No, cautious. Accustomed to keeping his cool until he's ready to push over the edge."

"You can push him first. What would *you* do? When he's kissing the sweet center of your palm, swirling his tongue over your ticklish flesh, how would you up the stakes?"

Danielle closed her eyes and conjured the scenario in her mind. Nick didn't come across as a sexual apprentice. The way he moved, the way he spoke, the way he grabbed her gaze with his and held it fast told her he was an undeniable master of the craft. Just how would someone with her varied, and yet limited, experience turn the tables to her advantage?

"I'd take his hand in mine and do the same naughty things to him."

"Is his palm smooth like yours?"

"No, rough," she guessed. "Callused and hard from holding heavy tools. Maybe scarred, too. Except the very center, right where the line of life on his palm starts to curve toward his wrist. Right there, he can feel everything twice as strong."

"How do you know?"

She found herself unable to answer Armand's question, instead enthralled by her own hand. She followed the three main palm lines with her fingertip. First, the line of heart and then the line of head. Last, the line of life. She followed each one, evoking new sensations. She licked her finger, then traced the lines again, imagining the spread of moisture came from Nick's tongue.

"Then what would he do?"

She wasn't sure, but she knew what she wanted.

"Undress me."

"Slowly?"

She shook her head. "No. His patience has limits. He'd rip off my clothes, then stop."

"Do as he would want, Danielle. Undress."

She wrangled out of her bra and panties. With a light touch, she dimmed the lamp and reclined on the couch, moving the phone so it was nearer to her mouth. She needed this fantasy, this release. She needed Nick, but if she couldn't have him, she'd settle for her only alternative.

"I'm naked."

"Lying down?"

"Of course. You?"

He groaned.

"Are you hard?" she asked.

Another groan.

She closed her eyes and Nick's image overpowered her mind. When she'd lived in Paris, she'd often watched Armand gratify himself. He'd demonstrated for her how to coax the most pleasure from his body. The memory should have popped into her mind with ease. Instead, she could clearly see Nick sitting on the edge of a rumpled blue bed, his cock in his hand, his cheek hugging the phone, his dark eyes staring into the shadows of his room.

"Talk to me," he said.

"I want your hands all over me," she admitted, skimming her palms up and down her legs.

"Where?"

"My breasts," she said, cupping them, running her thumbs around the tight centers, cooing as the sensations made her heavy and hot.

"Where else?"

"Oh, don't stop." She licked her fingers, then plucked her nipples to firm points. She stroked them mercilessly until her intimate lips throbbed to the beat of her heart.

"Your breasts are perfect. They taste like heaven."

She licked her fingers again, surprised at how easily she could recreate the sensation of his mouth on her breasts. He'd be gentle, but greedy. He'd suck and lick and bite until she cried out for him to stop. But he wouldn't stop. Not until she speared her fingers into his hair and dragged his lips away.

"I can't stand it, Danielle. I need to be inside you. I can't wait."

"Don't wait."

In her fantasy, he didn't wait. She spread her thighs for him, welcoming him, and in a flash of need, he swiftly pressed his hardness into her. Deeply. Completely. Her fingers mimicked what her mind saw. Her skin flamed and colors danced inside her eyelids. Yes. This was what she needed. What she wanted. Nick. Her Nick.

"Nicholai."

The lines between reality blurred and Danielle gasped as her fingers seemed to thicken inside her. She flicked the edge of her clit with her nail, sending herself into a spiral she couldn't resist. She called out his name, reaching deeper, knowing she would take this fall. The tumble would set her free.

Her body shook as she crossed the line. Slowly, the light returned to the room and the temperature, which had been so hot, now spawned a field of gooseflesh over her exposed skin. She grabbed the comforter and threw it over her, then reached for the phone. Before she spoke, she disengaged the speaker feature.

"Ar—"

Dial tone.

Weird.

She clicked the phone off, but didn't have the energy to call back. All she wanted now was a shower and bed. He'd call her tomorrow at lunchtime and they'd have a good laugh over the intensity of their transatlantic encounter. She glanced at the perfume bottle still nestled in the wooden box, but decided she wouldn't touch it again until after she'd had a good night's rest. She'd finally worked off a bit of her pent-up sexual energy. The gift's effect on her, whatever it was, would likely prove to be nothing more than her overactive imagination.

A sound drew her to the window on the other side of the room. She lived in the third-floor apartment of a home owned by Micki's brother-in-law, Alec Manning, and with no outside access except the front and back doors on the ground floor, Danielle usually left her window open during the day when she turned off her air conditioner. Had she forgotten to close it tonight when she'd come in?

The blinds fluttered. A tingle of electricity crackled around Danielle, so she hugged herself as she shot forward to find out what the hell was going on. She grabbed the cord and yanked the blinds noisily out of her way, just in time to see someone dart slowly but steadily across the front yard.

She leaned over the threshold. "Hey, you! Stop!"

The neighborhood surrounding Danielle's Lincoln Park apartment, just a block from an El stop and a short walk to DePaul University, was rarely quiet. The sidewalks, well lit and constantly traveled, snaked in front of the house, now silvery pink in the glow of the streetlamps. Yet Danielle couldn't get a good look at the person making her way so quickly away from the house. Definitely female. She'd seen skirts. The woman disappeared into the shadows of a truck parked on the street and then, seemed to vanish into thin air.

Danielle ducked back inside, closed the window and locked it tightly. For all she knew, the trespasser could have been someone innocently out in her robe searching for an errant cat. Danielle wasn't exactly quiet during her climaxes, but she doubted she'd attract attention from the street three stories down. The thought of someone eavesdropping on her phone call with Armand from that distance seemed ridiculous.

And so what if they had? Sometimes, you had to take the thrill however you could get it. With that defiant thought, warmth spread over Danielle like syrup on buttered pancakes, sweet and decadent. Fantasizing about Nick had been nothing short of delicious. How indulgent would the real thing be?

The question lingered, ripe with sensual speculation, until Danielle realized that while her self-gratifying adventure had sated her libido for the moment, she would see Nick live and in person first thing tomorrow morning. Would he know what she'd done? Would he somehow use those hypnotic black eyes of his to discover her secret fantasy? Was his mysterious, exquisite gift in any way connected to the overwhelming rush she'd been unable to fight?

With one last blast of rebellion, Danielle tore off the comforter before she shut the blinds. Sex didn't scare her anymore, and her sexuality was no longer a weakness she allowed men to exploit. What she did, she did by choice. Naked, she marched into the bathroom and turned on the shower to full-blast.

She wanted Nick Davis in her bed. She had since the first moment they'd met. So what was holding her back? Her job? So what if she suffered from a mild case of distraction over the next few days. She was the boss. Now that she'd approved the design of the first bed, she had the project completely under control. She deserved a few days of blissful preoccupation with her hunky carpenter, right?

She stepped into the scalding stream of water and braced herself while the heat worked its magic over her muscles and skin. Magic. She thought of the perfume bottle, wondering again if and how the objet d'art had influenced the night's events. Danielle wasn't one to believe in things she couldn't hold, taste or see firsthand, but she couldn't deny that the moment she'd opened the carved box, she'd been overcome with desire. The bottle's presence had acted like an amplifier of the lust and need she'd been trying to deny for weeks. And it wasn't just because she was impressed by his gift-giving skills. There was more to the present, she was sure. But what? She didn't have a clue.

But tomorrow, she'd find out.

4

"SHE STANDS OUT in a crowd, doesn't she?"

Nicholai looked up at the petite, redheaded waitress and wondered how the hell she'd known exactly what he'd been thinking. He'd been sitting beside the window of the coffee shop for a full fifteen minutes, allowing his espresso to cool while he watched Danielle across the street. He'd caught sight of her the minute she'd come marching around the corner from her train stop in her favorite spike-heeled boots, cell phone clutched against her ear and her eyes blazing with rage. She'd stopped at the front steps of the construction site, foregoing her usual detour to the coffee shop for her morning blend, and proceeded to confront some man in a suit carrying a polished briefcase and two sets of blueprints. He seemed to want to go inside the building, but Danielle wasn't rolling out the welcome mat.

The waitress narrowed her gaze, ducking down so she could see more clearly around the lettering on the other side of the glass.

"Do you know the man?" Nicholai asked.

The waitress shrugged. "Never seen him. Probably some unfortunate sap who caught Danielle before her first cappuccino. Poor guy. Hope he has good health insurance, because if he doesn't back up soon, she's going to kick him off the curb.''

Without bothering to laugh at her own joke, the waitress delivered the warm pastry he'd ordered and then sauntered back behind the counter. Though Nicholai's work was normally across town in his workshop, he'd be at the main job site today to deliver the first bed as he'd arranged with Danielle.

She'd opened his gift last night, he was sure. She must have unleashed the magic by now. How had it affected her? How had she reacted? He'd been haunted by a strange dream of them speaking on the phone, engaging in a sexual play of words and masturbation he'd read about, but had never tried. Would she be so adventurous? He'd desperately wanted to cruise by her apartment early this morning, but he'd decided to wait a few more hours, when the crossing of their paths wouldn't be so out of the ordinary.

He couldn't move too quickly, despite how the magic, once unleashed, would surge, then slowly weaken. He didn't have much time, but if he scared her, she'd never open her mind to the possibility that her soul and the soul of his lost wife were one and the same.

But one last glance out the window proved that her encounter with the magic last night hadn't slowed Danielle one bit. Even the construction supervisors— large men wearing hard hats and carrying sharp and heavy tools, who'd been blocking the entrance to the restaurant prior to her arrival—were taking slow but certain steps backward, out of Danielle's line of fire. With other women, the men might have jumped to her defense, offered her their protection from the guy with the briefcase. With Danielle, their instincts obviously told them to back off and remain at a safe distance.

Nicholai grinned and sipped his cold coffee. Some things never changed.

He tore into the glazed pastry, enjoying the sugary flavors. He thought about all the similarities between Danielle and Sofia. He did this every so often, listing all the clues he'd gathered to solidify his belief that his wife had been reincarnated. Just a month ago, he'd been so certain. He'd moved from Georgia to Illinois, created a new identity for himself and manipulated his way into Danielle's employ all for the sake of a belief that went against everything he'd ever been taught as a child, everything he'd ever learned as an adult.

How could she be Danielle and Sofia at the same time?

So far, he'd seen only glimpses of Sofia, but he'd learned so much about the woman who was Danielle. She was strong, sassy, smart-mouthed and intelligent. She had a dark past that spawned the whispers of the people around her, but she didn't seem to care about their speculative discussions or conjectural stares. She was incredibly comfortable in her new skin and for this, Nicholai was grateful. He desperately wanted her to acknowledge the life she'd had before with him, but not at the cost of the life she'd built for herself here and now.

"Do you know Danielle?"

The waitress had returned, and without his request, proceeded to replace his cold coffee with a hot cup. He didn't like the way her eyes swept over him with a flash of disdain he'd neither earned nor appreciated, but she'd definitely caught his interest.

"Do you?" he asked.

The girl's brown eyes sparked, but she attempted to hide the reaction by looking down and wiping his table.

"Sure, she comes in every morning."

"Oh, I thought you might be a friend of hers or something," he said, ducking beneath the curtain of her ponytail to catch her expression. He wouldn't have minded a little firsthand insight into Danielle, and this young woman seemed the perfect type to pump for information. She seemed wary, but hungry for attention. She had, after all, initiated this conversation. Perhaps she was anxious to show off that she was intimately associated with someone as important and impressive as Danielle Stone.

"Sure, we're friends." Her tone was resolute, her arms crossed. "We hang out. We went shopping last week at lunch. Bought purses, if it's any of your business."

Nicholai sat back into the cool leather of the booth. Yes, she was exactly what he needed.

"How do *you* know her?" the waitress asked, hands on hips.

Hmm. Protective, too. Interesting.

"I work for her," he answered. "I'm one of the contractors on the project."

Her eyes widened for an instant before she looked him up and down again, obviously trying to discern the truth of his story.

"I've never seen you before," she snapped, her tone

accusatory. "*All* the workers come in here for coffee in the morning."

He carefully injected his answer with a smile. "I don't work at the job site, usually. I'm building the...furniture."

Nicholai chose his words. He, like every other contractor or craftsman hired by Danielle Stone, had signed an agreement promising confidentiality in regards to the unique concept, menu and marketing strategy of the new restaurant. In a city like Chicago where world-class restaurants were as plentiful as skyscrapers and gentrified neighborhoods, a place like Pillow Talk needed to burst on the public scene in a big way. The investors, primarily Sebastian Stone, had insisted on secrecy from everyone associated with the project. Of course, when Danielle had broached the topic with him, he hadn't had a clue what she was talking about. He'd studied modern culture and did a fairly decent job of blending in, but marketing strategies were a bit beyond him. But a few pointed questions had given him a chance to absorb the information she'd explained.

She could be so different from his Sofia, who'd had no head for business. He could never even count on his wife to collect the takings at her performances in their traveling show. She'd had no head for numbers, no desire to make money. Sofia could be formidable when someone threatened to hurt her friends or her family, but otherwise was entirely nonconfrontational. Danielle, on the other hand, seemed to like a good fight.

With guarded gestures, Danielle finally convinced the man across the street to leave the premises. Nicholai watched him reach into his pocket as he retreated and wipe his sweaty brow with a handkerchief. Danielle, in response, stood on the bottom step of the entryway, her arms crossed, flanked on either side by her brawny soldiers. A feminine Napoleon.

Little details like that threw him off, made him wonder if the reincarnation theory he'd clung to wasn't just wishful thinking. But Danielle didn't just resemble his Sofia—they were exactly the same physically from the unique shade of their almond-shaped blue eyes to the pinpoint-sized mole at the base of their throat. Such details couldn't be attributed to mere coincidence. More like fate.

"Well, I'd better get back to the counter," the waitress said.

"Wait," Nicholai implored, curving his grin into a sultry smile. "You've piqued my curiosity."

The waitress twisted her mouth and stared at him with narrowed eyes. "About what?"

Obviously, his grin didn't pack the power it used to. "Your name."

The twist in her lips tightened. "Margo."

"Thanks, Margo. The coffee here is delicious. Pastry isn't bad, either. Even the company is first-rate. I'll have to stop in again sometime."

She shrugged her shoulders, mumbled a thanks, then stepped back to the counter to help a three-person queue of coffee drinkers waiting to pay for their morning fix. Nicholai sipped his espresso. Either he was losing his touch, or Margo was immune to the legendary Nicholai Vaux charm. Neither possibility thrilled him.

The door opened behind him and a blast of hot air shot into the room. Combined with the jangle of the overhead bell, the sensations seemed to send him back in time, to where a tin coffeepot hung over a fire on a sultry summer morning. Performers and craftsmen of his clan bustled to pack up their wares and move on to another town, another village, another *gaujo* enclave where he and his Romany brothers could collect another hatful of coins.

"Nick?"

He glanced up, startled. Danielle stood above him, her dark hair windblown and her skin flushed, likely from the altercation across the street.

"Danielle," he said, jumping to his feet. "I didn't see you come in. Can I buy you a cup of coffee? You look like you need one."

She grinned, but the smile was almost reluctant, as if she was happy to see him, but didn't want to be. "I never turn down free anything. A leftover from my previous life."

He moved toward the counter, but Margo, the waitress, waved from a distance at Danielle and pointed toward the cappuccino machine, ignoring the next patron in line.

Danielle gestured her thanks, then slid into the seat across from him, seemingly grateful to the preferential treatment she received from the adoring Margo.

Adoring. A strange word to choose, Nicholai thought, and yet, the perfect word.

"So, what are you doing here?" Danielle asked.

"Traffic was horrible, so I came ahead of the truck and told my driver to hold back until rush hour passed.

In the meantime, I figured I could find out where you wanted us to set up the bed. I can prepare the space myself.''

Her smile verified his guess that she appreciated his attention to detail. ''Great plan. Thank you. Geez, I find myself wanting to thank you quite a bit lately.''

Her cheeks darkened and a soft flush crept up her slim throat.

''You opened my gift?'' he asked.

Suddenly, Margo was standing beside them, a frothy drink dusted with cinnamon clutched in her hand. ''He gave you a gift?''

Her tone was light, but curious. She wore a smile, but Nicholai noted that it did not quite reach the depths of her eyes.

Danielle reached out for the drink. ''Thanks, Margo. Mr. Davis here is the ideal contractor. I haven't even paid him yet and he's already providing business incentives.''

Margo eyed him with scrutiny again, but this time her glance was quick and noncommittal. Before she could comment, a middle-aged man in a business suit burst into the store and started detailing a rather complicated, but no doubt lucrative, order for a sales meeting in a building next door.

Margo obediently returned to the counter. Danielle grinned after her.

''She a friend of yours?'' he asked, wanting to verify the information the waitress had provided. He had an odd feeling about Margo, likely because of the slight hero-worship look he'd seen in the waitress's eyes.

''Yeah, sort of. We hook up at lunch a lot and shop

when we can. But mostly, we chat when I come in for my coffee. She's one of those bubbly people who just injects the morning with a little sunshine, even on chilly days, you know?''

Nicholai shrugged. That wasn't his impression of the woman. Yes, she'd greeted most of the customers with warmth, but he'd felt a definite chill when he'd asked about Danielle.

"She seems friendly enough," he said.

"A perfect personality for a job like this. She wouldn't get far on my side of the street, though."

Nicholai nodded. "I witnessed your confrontation. You seemed to hold your own. Who was that man with the blueprints?''

"Regulator," Danielle said, the word spitting from her mouth as if a bad taste accompanied it. She sipped her coffee before she explained further. "Or so he claimed. His credentials looked real, but we just had a visit from the Department of Buildings yesterday. He insisted there had been a mix-up and if I'd just let him do his inspection, he'd close out his file and leave us alone.''

"And you didn't do that," Nicholai said.

"What? Let him in?" Her anger bubbled up again. "Hell, no. I have a nose for bullshit. He was a spy."

"A spy?''

She glanced around. "Quite a few competitors are showing advance interest in Divine Delights," she said, using the public name for the restaurant, an alias for the more evocative and still secret Pillow Talk. Only a handful of the contractors had been brought into the loop about the entire concept, but as the builder of the beds, Nick had the "highest security clearance," as Danielle had put it. He wondered how she'd react when she discovered Nick Davis wasn't even his real name.

She took a sip of her coffee, then licked a line of white foam from her lips. Nick covered his reaction by downing the rest of his espresso.

"Bas warned me that some competitors and reporters might try to send in spies, either to ruin the advance speculation about the restaurant or to steal the concept right out from under us. That's why the security checks on all of the workers have been so extreme."

Nicholai nodded. As someone with a completely fake identity, he'd sweated through the verification process. Luckily, the shady gentleman who'd sold him his credentials had clued him in on how to effectively fill in all the gaps of having no past. Danielle's security was likely very good, but he imagined they were ill-prepared to ferret out the real name of a man who died in an unmarked grave in Georgia a century ago.

Nick toyed with the tiny handle on the cup. "No doubt if these people are persistent enough, they can pay off one of your workers to get the information they want."

She sipped again and nodded. "Yes, they could. This isn't Area 51 and we're talking about a restaurant, not an alien invasion. I've just got to do the best I can so the Divines can open their venue with as much fanfare as possible."

Silence reigned for a moment, giving Nicholai a precious moment to study her face at rest. She stared out the window toward the construction site, her blue eyes lost in the conflicts and challenges she faced. And yet, she didn't seem the least afraid. Only determined. Between sips of her coffee, she pressed her lips together, her jaw steady and strong. The soft dusting of makeup on her cheeks, mouth and eyes added a gentle beauty to her fierce expression.

His heart halted, skipped a beat, then slammed against his chest. If she wasn't his Sofia, then someone had played a horribly cruel joke. He had no illusions that Danielle possessed the same old-world sensibilities as his lost wife or that Danielle could slip back into the old life they'd once shared. She would be different, of course, because she'd been reborn into a new life, one a hundred years and a thousand miles away from their shared past. But with the perfume bottle and his own special brand of seduction, he intended to coax back the love they'd once shared.

He had to, or he might go insane.

She caught his eye then, and he realized she'd been watching him while he pondered the intensity of his need to find his Sofia. Had she spied his duplicity in his expression?

"Now, about the perfume bottle..." she began.

A lump formed in his throat. Did she know? Did she possess some residual gypsy power to read his mind? He coughed, his lips tightly pressed together, trying to give nothing away in case she'd simply made a lucky guess.

"What do you want to know?"

"Where did you get it?"

"From a friend."

"A female friend?" she asked, one eyebrow arched. She didn't exactly look jealous, but her interest was aroused. He hated to disappoint her with the truth, but he knew his honest answer was more compelling than a lie.

"No, actually," he said, toying with the cardboard coaster beneath his coffee cup. "The bottle was given to me by a gypsy named Viktor Savitch."

"A gypsy?"

Nicholai nodded. For a moment, he considered how he could turn the conversation so that he didn't have to reveal so much right at this moment, but why should he delay? The truth was, he wanted Danielle. He knew she'd already unleashed the magic the bottle possessed. The magic was only temporary, so he didn't have time to waste.

"A Romany *sherrengro*."

"A what?"

He swallowed his disappointment that she didn't recognize the word. "A chieftain, a gypsy king, so to speak."

Danielle sat up straighter, recognition dawning in her blue eyes. Did she know? Had the mere mention of their ethnicity provided the stimulus for her memory?

"Wait, you're a gypsy, too," she said, understanding dawning in her gaze.

"Yes, I am Rom."

"Wow."

Her focus suddenly turned inward. What was she thinking? Was she remembering?

"No wonder you're so talented," she continued. "You probably have skills handed down from generations of craftsmen."

He only nodded, trying to hide another wave of disappointment. Why did he keep hoping she'd remember him? Why did he expect the love they'd shared to transcend the realities of life and death? Their love hadn't saved Sofia's life, had it? Their love hadn't barred him from being accused of her murder.

Nicholai palmed his scrunched napkin and stood to toss it in the trash can beside them. Then he dug a few bills out of his pocket and placed them on the table underneath the sugar dispenser. "I should get to the warehouse. The truck should arrive at any moment."

"Wait!" She grabbed her bag and joined him near the door. "You don't think I'd let you get away with that, do you?"

"With what?" he asked.

"Dropping a bomb on me. Several bombs. First, you give me a gift that isn't exactly what it seems, and then you tell me it was given to you by a gypsy king. To top it all, you admit to me that you're gypsy yourself. I need further explanation, mister."

Forever curious. Why wasn't he surprised?

"What more explanation could you possibly need?"

She grabbed his arm and before he could react, had dragged him out of the coffee shop and onto the sidewalk. Between the blare of car horns, the rumble of truck engines and the bang and whir of construction across the street, the noise was deafening.

And yet, he heard every word she said as if she'd whispered them intimately in his ear.

"I want to know what your gypsy king friend did to that bottle…or more importantly, what it's done to me."

5

"SO WHAT'S THE DEAL with the bottle?"

With the bed scheduled to arrive at the job site in minutes and the possibility of spies lingering as the most unusual piece of furniture was about to be delivered, Danielle had decided they should talk in her office. Situated in a corner near the kitchen, the small but functional room provided the one thing that was hard to come by on a construction site—privacy. She shut the door and dropped the blinds over the window that would soon be replaced with a two-way mirror so the restaurant manager could watch the customers and staff.

Nick grabbed a folding chair from the corner, flipped it around and sat. The move was typically cocky and male, and yet, she couldn't help but fight to stop a little breathy sigh from escaping.

"The deal?" he asked.

She eased around to her chair, slapping away the construction dust with her hand before sitting. "I mean, it's beautiful. Unique. Handcrafted."

His grin reached his fathomless black eyes. "I knew you'd appreciate it."

"As an artist, you mean," she said, testing him.

"As a woman."

Pass.

She lifted her bag onto the table in front of her. She wasn't exactly sure why she'd brought the bottle with her today, but she'd been halfway down the stairs of her apartment when a sense of loss had filled her. She'd known instantly that her connection to the bottle was to blame. She'd slept like a rock last night, but in the morning, she'd remembered snatches of a few vivid dreams. Some of the visions she'd recognized from her past. Faces of dealers. Memories of bone-chilling cold. Endless hunger. Other flashes of scenes were completely foreign. A hillside in the moonlight. Swimming naked in a stream.

Making love to a dark-haired man beneath a starless sky.

"Not all women like pretty things," she claimed, fortifying herself in order to ask him what she desperately needed to know, no matter how outrageous she knew her question would sound.

"Name one who doesn't."

Danielle quirked her lips, wondering why she couldn't come up with a name quickly. A few months ago, she might have volunteered Micki's name, but since taking up with her brother, who was richer than God, Micki Carmichael had definitely developed a taste for the finer things in life.

"Okay, you've got me, there. But that's not why you gave me the perfume bottle, Nick. I mean, that isn't the sort of gift you give to a business associate. A box of chocolates, maybe. A honey-baked ham during the holidays. Those are your standard, kiss-ass gifts. This goes above and beyond."

Nick's grin eased across his face and made his eyes sparkle with what she knew was pure male pride. "Then you liked it."

"Of course I liked it. So not the point."

"Then what is the point, Danielle? What has you so curious that you've called me into your office and ensured privacy in order to discuss it with me?"

Why did his description of what she'd done to arrange a few moments of uninterrupted conversation sound so lurid on his lips? So deliciously intriguing?

"The point is," she said, her voice strong and surprisingly steady, "I need to know why you gave me a gift so precious, so…intimate?"

Nick leaned forward. In the bright light of the office, she could see the scars on his hands, the calluses on his fingers. Last night, she'd imagined what his rough skin would feel like against hers. Today, she could find out.

"It's just a perfume bottle."

His answer snapped her brain out of its insane sensual suppositions. She snorted at his ridiculous claim. "Yeah, and you're just a carpenter."

He leaned back again. "I am just a carpenter."

She nearly dropped her bag. "My ass. You're an artist whose medium happens to be wood. You've also admitted to me that you're a gypsy and that the bottle was given to you by a gypsy king, which implies you have contacts with a world few people understand."

His eyebrows raised. *Good.* She liked that she'd surprised him. She knew next to nothing about the Romany, but she'd picked up a few facts here and there, mainly on the streets after she'd run away from home.

Runaways tended to develop a fascination with this culture, which was based on a nomadic existence.

"What do you remember about the Romany?" he asked.

Remember? What an odd choice of words. "Not much. I know you don't like to live in one place for too long. And that possessions are not of primary importance to you. That's why I'm so fascinated by the idea of you owning the bottle."

Nick relaxed, his mouth curled into a shape she'd best describe as a frown, though she couldn't be sure. "I never owned the bottle."

"Then how could you give it to me?"

"With permission, of course."

"Permission from the gypsy king?"

He nodded.

"Is he your king?"

Nick laughed, the sound throaty and loud. "A king is only necessary when there is a clan to rule. My clan died out years ago. Viktor Savitch is merely a friend."

Danielle tapped her fingertips on the top of her desk. Why couldn't she just get to the point? Why couldn't she just ask him point-blank what the bottle did? She'd never cared before if other people thought she was crazy, even in serious need of professional intervention. Which, after all, had turned out to be true. Perhaps she feared that acknowledging aloud that she believed the bottle was more than a knickknack for a vanity table represented a slip in her recovery, a chink in the chain of mental health she'd worked so hard to recover.

Of course, she was never diagnosed with anything beyond a drug addiction, stemming from a general and persistent feeling of disconnection from her family. And since rehab, she'd stayed off the drugs. As far as she knew, she no longer suffered from delusions or hallucinations. What she'd experienced last night after she'd opened the gift had been real.

She opened her bag and took out the carved box, which she had wrapped in a mismatched collection of tissue paper that she'd kept from her welcome-home gifts. She watched Nick as she peeled away the layers of crinkled pink, red and purple tissue, and witnessed the tightening of his knuckles once she revealed what she'd brought with her.

"You brought the bottle to work?" His glance darted over his shoulder toward the closed door.

Interesting. Maybe the gypsy king hadn't willingly handed over the bottle to give to her. Maybe it was stolen.

"I know enough about objets d'art to guess how priceless this perfume bottle might be. You didn't expect me to leave it at home, did you?"

She toyed with the clasp with her fingernails.

"It's a private gift, Danielle."

"I see that. Actually, I experienced the intimacy of the bottle's presence firsthand last night."

When she released the lock, Nick sprang to his feet.

"Not here," he insisted.

She stood, canting toward him, her hands braced on either side of the still-unopened box.

"Why not?"

He leaned in ever closer. She could smell the rich, nutty aroma of coffee on his breath. "I don't know what will happen."

Despite her instinct not to retreat, his admission pushed her back into the seat. "What do you mean?"

Nick hitched his hip onto her desk and gingerly laid a hand over the top of the box. He eyed her through those sinfully dark lashes. "You'll think I'm crazy."

She shrugged, trying to ignore the tingle of awareness glittering through her body. "Sane people scare me."

His expression was doubtful. "Do you believe in magic?"

"No."

He nodded, smiling, but more with irony than humor. "Do you believe in fate?"

He had her there. Yes, Danielle did believe in destiny, fate and all the accompanying notions surrounding predetermined directions for life and love. Perhaps it had been her unqualified belief in karma that had led her down such dark and dangerous paths up until now. For her entire life, she'd felt as if she were swimming upstream, struggling against currents with no instinct for direction. She'd never fit in, never had a place. Never knew what anyone wanted from her, like an alien in a lost world.

"What does fate have to do with this bottle?" she asked.

Nick shifted so he could pull his wallet out of his back pocket. From within the folds, he retrieved a folded piece of paper, which he opened then put down on top of the box.

It was a picture of her.

"Where did you get this?"

"From *Entrepreneur* magazine. They did an article on your brother a few months ago."

She snatched up the picture, which showed Bas at the bottom of the stairs leading from his private jet, holding out his hand to her as she walked down. When had this shot been taken? She recognized the clothes, a sapphire silk blouse Armand had sent her from Paris to celebrate her decision to work for Sebastian. This had been taken just after she'd signed on to work on Pillow Talk, when Bas and Micki had taken her to New Orleans to celebrate.

The day had been calm and sunny and the picture actually wasn't a bad one, despite the telephoto lens the photographer had undoubtedly used to get this close to her brother. Bas wasn't a recluse, but he guarded his privacy with fierce determination.

"I heard about the article, but I never saw it," she said.

"It was quite complimentary."

"What does the photograph have to do with me? What are you? Some sort of stalker?"

He laughed and Danielle couldn't deny the genuine sound. "You have no idea how often I've asked myself that very same question. However, since I have no intention of harming you or causing any unnecessary disruption to your life, no, I don't think I am. Not by the strictest definition."

"Then what are you?"

"A man who isn't the type to let a unique opportunity pass him by. The article wasn't just about your brother. There was a note about how you were overseeing his latest investment, his first foray into the restaurant business. They spoke about construction and I have a talent with wood. I am also a man in search of…a piece of my past. You, believe it or not, may be my key."

Danielle watched him carefully at the same time that she paid very close attention to her body's reactions. One of the reasons she'd survived five years of living on the streets was that she had incredible instincts—especially when she was clean and sober, like now. She could watch a person, tell when they were lying, when their concepts of reality split from the norm.

Nick Davis wasn't crazy. But he was crafty. And determined. She could see the resolve in the dark depths of his eyes, and the intensity of his gaze enhanced the persistent tingle that crackled between them.

"The key? What does that mean?"

He stood, crossed around the desk and nudged the chair she sat in away from the desk so he could barge into her personal space. She stood and spun around, bracing her hands behind her. With only inches separating them, Danielle could feel the heat emanating from his body, could smell the musky, woodsy scent of his skin. Close-up, his eyes captured hers and she couldn't bear to tear her stare away.

"It means, I'd like for us to get to know one another again."

"Again?" She managed to croak out the word, but had to swallow and focus before she could complete her thought. "Before you walked into my office a month ago, I'd never seen you before in my life."

"Are you sure?"

She saw him reach out, watched his hand slide toward hers, and yet she wasn't prepared for the jolt of electricity that sliced up her body the moment their flesh met. He brushed his palm up her bare arm, igniting a flame that instantly shot like bullets through her veins, blasting every nerve ending from the tips of her breasts to the pleasure point between her thighs. Her chest tightened, and knowing she couldn't deny what she so desperately wanted, she closed her eyes and waited, breathless, for his kiss.

She had no idea what he meant about her being the key to discovering some missing chunk from his past. She had no clue what he meant when he said he wanted to get to know her...again And right now, she didn't care. She simply wanted his lips on hers before her need to taste him drove her over the edge.

NICK KNEW HE SHOULDN'T. He couldn't. He would destroy his plan, his greater cause. And yet, he couldn't resist. He inhaled, and the breath seemed to draw her toward him until their lips parted, then met. An instantaneous flash of familiarity swam through him, and still, he couldn't close his eyes. He had to see her, watch her. The way her chin tilted to meet his. The way her lashes fluttered against the tops of her cheeks, dark and lacy. Yes, this was real.

The moment she slipped her hands around his waist, memories of the past flew from his brain. Her lips tasted sweet and frothy, her teeth smooth and clean. Her tongue tangled with his with complete confidence and keen exploration. When he took a half step forward, closing the energized space crackling between them, she groaned with need.

Awareness struck him, not only in the way her body responded to his like the strings of a guitar in the hands of a master musician, but awareness of who she was, who he was—where they were—together. Her breasts pressed against his shirt and she shifted her hips so that his hard sex curved into the soft concave of her belly.

Outside the office, something dropped. Banged. Splattered. Voices shouted and yet Danielle made no move to set him free. Instead, she dipped her palms over his buttocks and pulled him closer.

This wasn't the place or the time. But he couldn't stop, couldn't muster the self-discipline to deny what he'd craved for so long. His woman. His wife. His other half, reborn into someone he did not know.

Suddenly, she broke away. He didn't move, but realized his hands gripped the edges of her desk with such force, his joints ached. He locked his gaze on her face, enraptured by how she licked her lips, as if she simply had to have one more taste before she ended this interlude.

"Sorry about that," she said.

"Sorry about what?"

She pushed past his arm and instantly created a distance. "I shouldn't have let that happen. It's unprofessional."

"By whose standards?"

She bit her bottom lip. "Seems to me it's generally good business sense not to screw around with your employees."

"Technically, I'm not an employee," Nicholai said,

deciding to put some of his newly acquired business knowledge to good use. "I'm an independent contractor."

"You also might be delusional," she cracked.

He couldn't deny that. "A distinct possibility."

She crossed her arms over her chest. "Then why aren't my instincts telling me to run?"

He ventured a guess. "Because you're not the type to run away when you're frightened?"

She shook her head emphatically. "See, there you go, showing how much you don't know me. I'm a world-class runner when it comes to escaping dangerous situations."

"I'm not dangerous."

"So you say."

"So I can prove."

"How?"

"Have dinner with me."

"What?"

He pushed off from the desk and though he skimmed into her personal space just long enough to stir the unnerving vibes bouncing between them, he walked back to the other side of the desk and returned to the chair there.

"Come to my loft tonight for a home-cooked meal and I'll tell you everything you need to know about me, the perfume bottle, my woodwork. Even my hopes and dreams for the future if you promise not to let me bore you to tears."

She inhaled, exhaled, pressed her lips together—but never took her eyes off his. She was considering his offer. Dare he hope? She had already opened the gift, thus releasing the magic Viktor had created with his charm. The gypsy king had warned him that the spell would not last indefinitely. Perhaps kissing her hadn't been in his initial plans, but her willing reaction spurred him to press further, faster. He wanted his wife back. Why should he wait?

"I don't know."

He nodded. She hadn't declined, which was a success in itself.

"I'll take that as a maybe. My workmen must be here by now with the first bed, so I should go out and supervise the unloading. Where do you want it?"

Danielle listened to him, then shook her head as if she needed to clear her mind before she dealt with business. He'd thrown her off balance. Good. The spontaneous kiss had affected her. Excellent. His own blood was still thrumming, and the perspiration tickling him beneath his collar wasn't from the temperature of the room. Yet so long as they were equally overwhelmed, Nicholai could control the situation. He had to open her mind to the possibilities of the unexplained, and more importantly, the unbelievable.

With rapid movements, Danielle smoothed her hands down her blouse, straightening her clothing and marching to her desk to tap and stack an assortment of papers and file folders.

"Set up in the VIP room. I've already outlined the mural for that room so the Divines will see this afternoon what the rest of the restaurant will look like once the renovations are complete."

He shoved his hands in his pockets and nodded. "Will do."

He turned to leave, but she stopped him by calling his name.

"Yes?"

She gestured toward the box. "You should take that back. It's too valuable. I shouldn't have accepted it."

He threw a level stare in her direction. "Funny, I never would have expected you to fall prey to the dictates of someone else's sense of propriety."

She narrowed her gaze at him. "You're trying to manipulate me."

He grinned. "Is it working?"

"Why do you want me to have the bottle so badly?"

"The same reason you want so desperately to keep it. It intrigues you."

"It scares me."

"Nothing scares you."

She snorted, which made Nick laugh.

"You keep saying that and maybe I'll eventually believe you. But I'll keep it. For now," she conceded.

He turned toward the door.

"Good," he said under his breath.

For now would have to do.

6

NICHOLAI PUT DOWN his veiner gouge, his hands aching. He glanced at the clock, then blinked twice to make sure he wasn't imagining how long he'd been working—nearly six hours, nonstop. While not surprised that he'd gotten caught up in the task of carving a trellis of roses for the canopy of the next bed, he was surprised he'd lasted this long without his mind wandering to Danielle. Would she show up tonight? Would she bring the bottle? Would she be ready for him to finally reveal his secret?

Despite his doubts, he possessed confidence in his ability to seduce her into loving him again—a confidence that might just prove him a fool.

He'd spoken to her one last time before he'd left the construction site, promising her a fascinating evening if she decided to take him up on his invitation to dinner. Again, she'd been noncommittal, but her cheeks had flushed enough so that he knew she was seriously considering his offer. But now, it was past nine o'clock. What were the chances she'd come by for dinner so late?

Ten minutes after he'd cleaned his tools and returned them to his chest, the buzzer on the front door sounded.

Apparently, his chances weren't so bad.

He grabbed a rag on his way to the door and used the cloth to flick away the curls of carved wood clinging to his arms and clothes. He hoped she liked her dinner companions messy, because what she saw was what she got.

"Danielle?"

She grinned shyly at him, her hands engaged in balancing a thick pizza box. "Hope I'm not too late."

He opened the door wider so she could pass in front of him. Even the robust scent of garlic and onions couldn't overpower the subtle citrus of her perfume. She wore the same clothes she'd worn to the office today—slim jeans that hugged her hips, high, spike-heeled boots, a form-hugging black sweater with a silver zipper tracing up the front. Only she'd added a decorative scarf to the mix, one that instantly reminded him of the comforter he'd put on the first bed yesterday.

Had she consciously chosen it?

"Nice scarf."

She grinned, fingering the silk. "Like it? I saw it in a shop window today and I just had to have it. It's weird. I usually hate shopping."

He locked the door behind them, then gestured her into the workshop. "It suits you."

"Are you still hungry?" she asked, her eyes hopeful.

"I've been working nonstop for hours. I'd completely forgotten to eat."

"Perfect!" she said with a grin. "This is Chicago-style pizza. If you want more than one piece, you pretty much have to be ravenous."

The lighting inside the warehouse provided a glow-ing outline of her petite figure, from her trim waist to her soft shoulders and saucy swinging hips. Ravenous didn't begin to describe the ache in his belly.

She marched inside confidently, but stopped when she obviously wasn't sure just where in this cavernous space they would have dinner.

"Let me," he said, taking the pizza box from her. "We can eat in the little kitchen on the other side of that wall, if you'd like. It used to be the break room."

Danielle glanced around, her lips turned down in a little frown. Obviously, that didn't appeal to her.

"I also have a loft upstairs," he offered. "It's nothing fancy, but it's definitely sawdust-free."

She smiled. "That sounds great. I like a lot of stuff on my pizza, but wood chips isn't my favorite topping."

He chuckled and directed her to the concrete stairs that sliced up the back wall to the space he'd turned into his living area. More than likely used previously for storage, the loft was spacious and open, flanked on the side overlooking the warehouse by a sturdy wall of iron bars. From the loft, he could see over the entire warehouse, but with no risk of falling.

"This is cool," she said.

He'd filled the space with items best described as eclectic, but in truth, he'd purchased the furnishings because they'd been cheap or in some cases, free. He'd replaced the blinding, industrial light fixtures with mismatched ceiling fans. A dozen rugs, some faux animal skin, some thick and shaggy, covered the polished concrete floor he'd painted dark green. Muted gold light glowed across the space from two table lamps, but he had an expansive collection of candles and kerosene lanterns that probably defied some fire code, but made him feel more at home. He deposited the pizza on the low boxy table he'd found in the lobby of the building shortly after he'd moved in, then turned to retrieve a bottle of wine from the rack he kept in a cool corner.

"Do you own this place?" she asked, unwrapping the long silk scarf from around her neck.

"No," he said, choosing a hearty red from his collection. He and Jeta had done a bit of exploring on their way from Georgia to Illinois, one of their favorite discoveries being local wineries. Homegrown vintages reminded him of a life gone now for over one hundred years. He shook the brief shadow of melancholy away. Tonight was as much about the future as the past. "I leased the space with the help of a friend. The owner is considering bartering a renovation in exchange for rent, if I decide to stay."

She removed her large tote bag from her shoulder, the same bag she'd used to carry the perfume bottle to her office this morning. Did she still have the case with her?

His torso tightened from his chest to his groin. He hadn't considered the consequences of her bringing the magic back into his home. Hell, he hadn't considered the consequences of much beyond enticing her to remember who she'd once been. He retrieved the wine and a corkscrew, and decided simply to play the cards as they were dealt. And pray for a lucky hand.

She removed a stack of napkins from her bag, but he had to run downstairs to retrieve utensils and paper plates. He kept his wineglasses, a mismatched collection of four, with the wine. Soon, they were settled in for a meal at the low table, sitting on pillows and laughing over the overstuffed quality of good Chicago pizza.

"This is fabulous," he said, disconnecting a string of cheese from his chin.

"Yeah," Danielle agreed. "You don't get pizza like this in Paris."

Nicholai's eyes widened. While he hadn't spent much time in the City of Lights, France had been his playground in his youth. "You lived in Paris?"

She nodded, then picked a piece of sausage off her plate and popped it in her mouth. "For a little over a year. My brother sent me to rehab there."

He remembered reading that tidbit in the article about her, but the reporter hadn't provided much information. Nicholai had had to ask Evonne what the term "rehab" meant, and from her explanation, he figured Danielle would be much more discreet about the experience than to mention it so flippantly. He wondered if she opened up this way to everyone, or if her revelation to him meant something more intimate.

"That must have been hard," he said, sliding another slice of pizza from the thick cardboard box.

She shrugged. "Sometimes."

She glanced furtively at her wineglass. Nicholai suddenly realized she hadn't taken a single sip.

"Should you not drink?"

She closed her eyes and took a deep breath before answering. "You have no idea how hard it is. I mean, I'm not an alcoholic. I drank like everyone else on the streets, but my poison was drugs. When I got clean, I laid off everything that could be addictive. Except chocolate," she said with a smile. "Girl's gotta have some vices."

Nicholai nodded, then without a word, disappeared downstairs and reappeared with a cold bottled water. "You should have asked for another drink," he gently admonished her.

She cracked open the plastic bottle top. "I would have, eventually. I just came here with so many questions, I figured I should put them in order of importance."

He returned to his seat on the floor across from her. "Questions about the perfume bottle?"

She sipped her water, then wiped her mouth with a napkin. "Of course." Her eyes darted downward, as if she wasn't exactly thrilled with her curiosity.

He knew how she felt.

"Did you bring it with you?"

She glanced at her bag. "It's weird, but I don't want to leave it behind. I mean, I know it's very valuable, but that's not it. I feel, I don't know, connected to it."

So Viktor's magic was potent, just as his friend had promised.

"You *are* connected to it. The bottle is more than an objet d'art, more than a priceless antique from another age. You told me earlier that you don't believe in magic. Perhaps you should reconsider."

At his unspoken request, Danielle frowned, but scooted the bag toward him. He dug beneath the cushioning tissue and retrieved the wooden casket.

According to Viktor, when he'd been trapped in the bottle, the victim of a witch's black magic, the box had been sealed with a binding spell that ensured that the gypsy king wouldn't escape. Since Eve, Viktor's lover, had figured out how to counter the spell, the box now acted only to protect the perfume bottle and all the magic cradled within.

"Tell me everything you know about this bottle," Danielle requested, her voice breathy with expectation. "Where did it come from?"

Nicholai ran his hand over the carvings on the box, marveling yet again at the exquisite craftsmanship. "I don't know where or when the bottle was made, but back in the late-nineteenth century, it fell into the hands of a Romany family in England called Dulas."

"The Dulas?" She shook her head. "I've never heard of them."

"You wouldn't have. Romany history is not taught in schoolbooks, but it is handed down orally from clan to clan, generation by generation. My clan, for instance, wandered all of Western Europe during my lifetime, but reportedly, had come from a region in Russia. I grew up mostly in France."

Her eyebrows shot up. "In Paris?"

"Everywhere but Paris, I think. May have been there once, on the outskirts. I don't really remember."

"When did you come to America?"

Nicholai paused. He couldn't exactly answer 1890, now could he? "When I was twenty-five."

"How old are you now?"

"Thirty-five." Give or take one hundred years, though he figured the time between his murder and his crossover back into the world of the living shouldn't count.

She pressed her lips together, as if trying to decide whether or not to believe his story.

"You have no accent," she concluded. "Except when you say gypsy words."

He accepted her compliment with a smile. "I've lived many places."

"Gypsy wanderlust," she decided, hefting her pizza to her mouth and taking a generous bite. Something in his story must have clicked, because her wariness disappeared and was replaced by ravenous hunger.

He grinned wider, both at her appetite and her immediate understanding of his need to roam, move, explore. "We invented the concept, yes. It's believed the Romany actually began as a nomadic people from India, on an exodus to escape persecution. They told the *gaujo* they met on their travels that they were from mystical Egypt, a country more known in the Western world for exotic mysticism. The *gaujo* feared the gypsy and that fear kept the gypsies alive."

"Until they were persecuted in Europe as well."

Nodding, he chose to skip over the bloody past of his people. No need to rehash what was common knowledge, even today. "Sometimes, the gypsies persecuted each other. The Dulas family possessed the *bengesko yak,* the evil eye. They practiced black magic, which is forbidden among most gypsies. This bottle belonged to the Dulas family, and reportedly, they enchanted it with both a curse and a charm."

She pushed her plate away, wiped her mouth. Though her lips pressed together tightly, Nicholai could sense no disbelief or doubt in her expression.

Instead, she listened intently, her gaze locked on the wooden box he'd continued to caress with his hands.

"So it's both good and evil?" she asked.

"It was. My friend, Viktor Savitch, the gypsy king I told you about, was the grandson of a great *chovihano,* a Romany sorcerer and healer. Viktor was able to break the influence of the black magic and retain the white."

She chewed on her bottom lip, but scooted closer.

"What does it do?"

Nicholai inhaled a deep breath. This was it. The time had come. She hadn't recoiled from the story so far, and he had no reason to believe that revealing the truth would ruin the tenuous connection they currently shared. If he could coax her just a little farther, he'd soon be able to show her exactly how the box could help her—help them—rediscover their past.

"It acts as an amplifier to people with paranormal abilities. Someone who communicates with the dead, for instance, would be able to speak more clearly with them—even see them, touch them."

Her eyes met his, a slash of doubt marring the perfect blue color. "I don't have a paranormal ability. I'm not sure I even believe anyone does."

"But you don't disbelieve entirely, do you?"

She paused, then shook her head. She placed her hands on the table, palms down, but made no move to touch the box. "I guess anything is possible in this crazy world."

"And you've felt the power of the box, haven't you?"

She glared at him. "Why did you give it to me?"

"Because I wanted you to remember."

"Remember what? You keep saying that, and I don't know what you mean!" Suddenly, shock blanched her face. She scrambled to stand and Nicholai did the same. The fear in her eyes stabbed at his chest and for a moment, he thought her short raspy breaths might not be enough to keep her conscious.

"What is it, Danielle? Do you remember something?"

"Did I know you?" She croaked out the question as if her throat had tightened painfully. "Did I know you…before?"

Nicholai held his tongue. Her eyes told him she wasn't asking about France, about their marriage, about their lives in the caravan.

"Before…when?"

"When I was an addict, that's when. Living on the streets!" Her voice grew louder and more frantic, but she didn't retreat. He could see the bloody war raging between her fear and her need to discover the truth. "I've forgotten huge chunks of my life from that time, some by choice and some because I burned too many brain cells. But I have nightmares sometimes. Horrible, terrifying nightmares of men with faces I can't quite make out. Men who—"

Nicholai reached out for her, but was careful not to make contact, sensing she would pull away, perhaps even run, before he could explain.

"Don't, Danielle. I'm not one of those men, believe me. I think I did know you before, but not from Chicago. Not from the streets."

He watched her throat bob, her eyes grow glossy.

She blinked and plopped back down to the floor. She grabbed her water bottle off the table, but didn't drink. She merely played with the top, twisting it open and closed, open and closed, while the color returned to her face.

Nicholai cleared away the plates, napkins and pizza, giving her a moment to regain her composure. He knew next to nothing about her childhood as Danielle Stone. Before now, he frankly hadn't cared. But living as a gypsy by tradition and choice was very different from retreating from civilization as an outcast. He'd only recently learned about runaways, but the knowledge of their suffering had struck him deeply.

He'd met teenaged runaways on the sidewalks outside his warehouse. The dispossessed children camped out in the alleyways on either side of the building, panhandling for food and money, bartering with everything they possessed, which usually wasn't much but sometimes included their bodies. His grandmother, Jeta, had recognized the runaways for what they were—gypsies with no families to bind them, no culture to keep them safe. Lost, with no tradition to act as guide.

He couldn't imagine Danielle in their place. Homeless. Loveless. Alone, even in a crowd.

When he finally sat down beside her again, she'd wiped the moisture from her eyes. "I'm sorry, Nick. It's just that I don't see the faces when I dream. For all I knew—"

"I could have been someone who hurt you. I understand. Don't apologize. I had no idea you'd been a runaway. How did that happen? How did your brother let you live on the streets?"

With a sniffle, Danielle shook her head. "Bas never knew, not until after I was ready to get my act together. He's a lot older than me, nearly eighteen years. After he went off to boarding school and then college, he rarely came home. He hardly knew me. When he did call to check up on me, my parents lied and told him everything was fine, that I was doing great in school, that I was turning into a female version of him. None of it was true, of course. I ran away the first time when I was fifteen. I couldn't live up to what my parents wanted from me."

"To be like your brother?" he guessed.

He couldn't remember the last time he'd thought about his own mother and father. He'd moved out on his own at a young age and they'd eventually gone on to travel with a different clan. Jeta had raised him, and her expectations of him had been simple and easy to meet. Live. Love. Be kind. He couldn't imagine what Danielle had gone through, but he was eternally grateful that she was willing to tell him, at least in part.

She grabbed a throw pillow and hugged it to her chest. "That's just it. They told *him* they wanted me to be just like him, but they never told me. As far as I knew, they never expected me to turn into anything but a junior version of them—money-hungry and useless. They'd inherited every dime they had, and they went through money like water. Bas was a millionaire before he was twenty-five, so he supported us. I guess the 'rents realized they were lucky to have one genius in the family, so why put any expectations on me? They just bought my clothes, my toys and my silence."

"What about your love? Did they try to buy that as well?"

Danielle coughed, the sound a heart-wrenching mixture of sardonic humor and infinite sadness. "They never bothered. They never cared. As long as Bas continued to finance their parties and vacations, I didn't matter to them. I still don't matter, but now, it's okay. I matter to Bas. And I matter to Micki, his fiancée."

Nicholai shifted closer to her, laid his hand beside hers. "You matter to me."

"Why?" she asked, her gaze pointed and strong. "We're strangers."

"No, we're not."

The time had come. Nicholai scooted the box toward them, flicked the latch and opened the top. He scooped the bottle from its protective indentation in the scarlet satin, and held the phial toward Danielle, an offering of the unknown.

The perfume bottle gleamed, even in the dim light from the lamp. The facets seemed to absorb the tiny glimmers and reflect them back like sunbeams. Danielle's breath caught audibly and when he looked at her, her eyes had rounded into sapphire saucers.

"What will happen if I touch it again?" she asked, even as her hands slowly inched toward the bottle.

"You'll remember."

Or at least, he hoped she would, with all his heart and soul.

7

DANIELLE FILLED her lungs with air, hoping the oxygen would somehow increase her courage. Last night, after she'd touched the bottle, she'd experienced a completely overwhelming flood of desire. Her body, from deep within her skin, had flamed with a fire she now suspected wasn't entirely natural, but had definitely spawned from the instant attraction she'd felt toward Nick.

According to Nick's outrageous claim, she'd been under the influence of a paranormal amplifier, for lack of a better term. And while she knew she didn't possess any powers that couldn't be explained through simple science and common sense, she also knew she couldn't deny the inconceivable power of what she'd experienced—a pure, concentrated lust unlike anything she'd ever known.

And last night, she'd been alone with only Armand on the phone four thousand miles away. The true object of her desires had not been sitting right beside her, offering her a mysterious story she had no business listening to, much less believing. Magic didn't exist. People did not possess paranormal powers that couldn't be explained away as either tricks of modern technology or old-fashioned sleight of hand.

Did they?

She reached out to him, her hands cupped together, forming a safe cradle for the bottle. With an expressionless face, he placed the glass in her palms. Like last night, a tingle of warmth snaked up her arms, then coiled deep inside her, latching on to her with full force. She closed her eyes as a clash of sensations assailed her. Cold wind. Hot fire. Smells both sweet and fetid. Sounds that blared in her ears and whispered against her skin. The moment her lids dropped, a scene at once foreign and familiar came instantly into view.

A sky, ink-black with clouds. An umbrella of tree branches clawing above her, swaying in the wind of an upcoming storm. After a moment of incredible warmth, a cool breeze buffeted her body, naked, head to toe.

She could no longer feel the perfume bottle in her hands. She couldn't feel anything beyond the soft nip of coolness curling around her flesh, taunting her nipples into hard peaks, spawning a field of gooseflesh across her bare skin. She blinked, but the vision wouldn't clear. She managed only to say, "Nicholai?"

Nicholai? Not Nick? Was that her voice she'd heard?

No—two voices had answered simultaneously—both the same in depth and tone, but replying with different words. Her ears registered the distinct invitation of, "Over here, my love," while somewhere in the back of her mind, she heard the same man say, "Relax. It's only a very powerful vision. When you truly want to break the connection to the past, you will. You have the power."

Unsure, she tested what he said. She concentrated on what Nick's loft looked like, focused on her need to be free of the vision and suddenly, she could see him clear as day, sitting beside her on the floor, cupping his hands beneath hers in case she dropped the bottle. Her hands were shaking, but the bottle still glittered in her palms.

Light-headedness kept her eyesight slightly blurry and narrowed, as if the edges still possessed a connection to the vision from the past. She only had to look askance to jump back into the world she knew she'd never seen before.

"What just happened?" she asked.

"You saw the past."

"You were there?"

"Yes."

She shook her head. "I don't remember that place. I don't remember ever being naked outside just before a storm blew through. And it wasn't Chicago…or back home in Michigan."

Nick didn't move, but he licked his lips and cleared his throat as if his mouth was parched. "No, not Chicago or Michigan. But you do remember, deep in your soul. If you didn't, the bottle would not have been able to coax the memory from you."

So why did he look so disappointed? Wasn't this what he had wanted, for her to remember? He'd said so quite a few times, though always in a cryptic way that until this moment, Danielle had not understood. Hell, she still didn't understand.

"When was this…memory?" she asked.

"Many years ago."

"You're not that much older than me. *Many* years

ago, I was a baby and you were probably a snot-nosed kid.''

He cleared his throat again, but didn't crack as much as a grin at her remark. The hair behind her neck prickled. Just what had she seen?

''Danielle, this happened over a century ago.''

''What?''

With great care, Nick plucked the bottle out of her hands. The moment he broke the connection, Danielle's arms suddenly slackened, heavy with their own weight. He placed the bottle back in the box, but didn't shut the lid. Instead, his fingers toyed with the latch and his gaze seemed a million miles away. Or more appropriately, one hundred years away.

She rolled her shoulders and rubbed her arms until the blood flow returned and the tingle in her nerves began to dissipate. The bottle seemed to vibrate with a low-level electric current, one with a source she couldn't identify.

She'd had enough. Curious as she was about the true nature of the bottle, she wasn't a fool. She'd dealt with more than her fair share of uncertainty and confusion in her life. Why add more, all on account of a man? A sexy man, admittedly, but a man nonetheless.

''Nick, if you don't explain this to me right now, I'm out of here. You can keep your gift and your mysteries and your secrets. I'm not interested. I have enough trouble managing the things that happen to me on a daily basis in the real world. I don't need to dredge up some mysterious blocked memory you say I have, especially with the help of a bottle that can't possibly be doing what I can see with my own eyes that it is!''

Her rant did not seem to faze him until he turned to her, and for the first time since they'd met grabbed her without warning. He grasped her hands in his and proceeded to rub out the magical thrum with his palms, creating hot friction, replacing the mysterious tingle from the bottle with heat, elemental and instinctual.

God, she wanted him. With every fiber of all that made her feminine, she craved this man. She couldn't remember when she'd experienced desires so compelling, so powerful—so forbidden. Not because she didn't have complete control over what might happen, but because she had no idea what price she'd pay for crossing so deeply into the unknown.

She yanked away. She wouldn't be so easily diverted.

"You've got one shot here, Nick Davis." She jabbed her finger toward him to emphasize her point.

"My name is not Nick Davis."

Her breath caught, but the honesty in his eyes told her that fear wasn't the right reaction to his confession. What was a fake name in relation to the freaky scenario at hand? Besides, if he were going to hurt her, he would have done so already. And why would he have bothered to confuse her with some ridiculous story about one-hundred-year-old repressed memories?

"Then who are you?"

"My true name is Nicholai Vaux."

The name meant nothing—except from the vision.

"Are you really gypsy?" she asked, unable to put the pieces together without more information.

"Yes," he answered, his voice deep with sincerity.

"That part of the story, and all that I told you about Viktor, is true."

Her shoulders drooped forward, her spine a rope of taffy, unable to retain her posture while the story that Nick, er, Nicholai, told grew wilder and weirder. She'd called him Nicholai in the vision—before she'd even known his real name.

"I don't understand," she admitted, crumbling to the ground and cradling her head in her hands. She was glad he'd cleared away the wineglass, because at this point, temptation might have gotten the best of her.

From above her, he cursed under his breath in a language Danielle realized she didn't know. Still, his frustration was clear.

"How can you understand?" he spat, his ire aimed clearly at himself. "I've gone about this completely wrong! You have to know, I have no more experience than you do. How do you tell someone something you know they will not believe, and yet, that you know is the truth?"

He knelt beside her, his words a warm entreaty against her ear. "You've seen the magic, Danielle. You know the power of the vision. And from what you've told me tonight about your past, you know the difference between a hallucination and what the bottle gave you."

He was right. Danielle did know the difference all too well. Drug-induced hallucinations varied from person to person, from trip to trip, but some aspects didn't change. For one, they didn't turn on and off in a split second. And most of the time, once she came out of the stupor, she couldn't remember a single thing she'd reportedly seen or done or said while under the influence. She used to laugh like hell when she'd wake up and Micki would tell her all the wild things Danielle had said she'd seen.

She wasn't laughing now.

No, what she'd experienced tonight, however briefly, had not been the result of drugs, and from her experience in rehab, she knew she was immune to hypnosis. She couldn't find a single logical explanation for the power and clarity of the vision she'd seen except... The magic was real.

"How can I have a hundred-year-old memory?" she asked, snapping her gaze to him.

He didn't blink. "Do you understand the concept of reincarnation?"

He spoke so calmly, so rationally. She stared at him, dumbstruck. Reincarnation? God, were her instincts so far off that she'd fantasized about a man who was certifiable?

"Are you talking about past lives?" she asked.

He nodded, but she could see the reluctance in his grimly drawn lips and serious eyes.

She pressed a hand to her heart, trying to steady what was becoming a very rapid pulse rate. "You expect me to believe that you and I knew each other in another lifetime? That we're reincarnated soul mates?"

"Oh, no," he insisted, chuckling uncomfortably. "I expect you to think I'm nuttier than a candy bar." He reached for her, palms out, but didn't touch her. He simply left his hands there, open, offered—for her to take or deny as she wanted. "But there are a lot of very respected, very intelligent, very *sane* people who do believe that reincarnation is just another facet of spiritual existence.''

She reared back. ''So just because some wack jobs with high IQs believe that they were once Napoleon or Shakra the Viking in a former life, I'm supposed to take your word that reincarnation is real?''

He inched closer to her, but didn't break the invisible boundary she'd built with her anger.

''I wouldn't dare broach the topic with you if I couldn't prove my case,'' he said.

''Prove it?''

Her hands ached to slide into his, but she balled them into fists and concentrated on keeping them at her sides. Why did she want to trust him so badly? Was she still vulnerable from rehab? Was she so sex-starved she couldn't tell the difference between trust and attraction?

Or did she, deep inside, simply have some inkling that what he claimed could be true?

His wild theory would explain so much. All her life, she'd felt out of time, out of place. With her parents, her classmates, her neighborhood friends. Her mother and father had filled her bedroom with everything a wide-eyed, pink-loving little girl could want—and yet, whenever they'd shut her door, she'd felt like a feather stuffed inside a plump pillow. Outside, in the open air, she'd discovered a hint of relief. Yet, there were always gates, always fences.

The drugs she'd started to take when she was twelve had helped a little. The weed took the edge off the long nights in her canopy bed filled to the four posters with Gund bears and collectible Barbie dolls. From there, she'd experimented with the gamut of easy-to-get narcotics, from Ecstasy to GHB. And yet, the drugs hadn't been enough to quell the restlessness that haunted her.

So she'd run away from home, certain she'd find the freedom she craved on the streets of a glamorous, cosmopolitan city like Chicago, where she could blend into the mass of humanity. She'd learned to survive on her own, but only by trading her soul for an occasional hit.

In rehab, she'd finally realized that the discontent she'd sought to ease with drugs had haunted her all her life and that her parents' careless attitude toward her upbringing wasn't entirely to blame. She'd always known there was something more, something deeper, some missing link buried so completely inside her, even she couldn't access it. Was her distant past the explanation for her restless wandering and constant questioning? If she followed where she believed Nick was going with his claim—that she possessed a soul lost in the great mystery of time and space—would that explain why she'd never felt at home anywhere, with anyone?

She grabbed the bottle out of the box and clutched it to her chest. The tendrils of sizzling sensation struck her between her breasts and the vision exploded into her brain with an audible hiss. A light flashed and then she was back in the starless night.

She calmed her rapid breathing and soon, sounds trickled into her ears that solidified the vision. Crickets. The spiraling whistle of wind through the trees. The rustle and crunch of leaves. The rush of water over stones.

The minute the noises registered, Danielle's toes tickled from the cool water lapping over them. The wind again played with the nakedness of her body and tossed long hair in dark streaks across her face. She pushed her hair back and with eyes now adjusted to the golden glow of a kerosene lamp attached to a branch on a tree, she caught site of Nick.

But not Nick. Nicholai. Dressed in black trousers, a green silk shirt embroidered with blue thread and tall, worn boots. He wore an earring, as he did in the present, but instead of the subtle emerald, it was a large, shiny hoop.

He tore the ring from his ear and tossed it to the ground, then unbuckled his boots, standing and hopping on one foot.

"I found you," he said, his voice triumphant.

Danielle experienced the strangest sensation as laughter bubbled up inside her, then erupted like music into the night. She watched Nicholai hop around and undress with eyes that saw none of the graceless silliness, but only the humor and fun. In an instant, she realized the emotion that clouded her view.

Love.

Deep, intense love.

Before she could retreat from the scene again, he was undressed and splashing across the brook toward her. She felt herself turn and run, but with no intention of escape. The tease intensified the dark look of complete desire she witnessed in Nicholai's gaze the moment he snatched her into his arms.

"You don't think I'd allow you to escape now, do you?"

God, his eyes were darker than the night, yet his smile gleamed with the light of his desire. He pressed her full against him, his erection stiff against her belly, making her sex weep for his.

"Don't you dare let me go," she heard herself command, watching as her fingers speared into his hair, disappearing into the silken strands.

He kissed her then, hard and long and wet. Their mouths melded, hands roamed, searched, pleasured. By the time she'd stroked him to full, impressive length, a pearl of moisture spilled from the tip of his cock and with a shock, Danielle realized she wanted nothing more than to lick it away.

She didn't have the chance. Nicholai lifted her into his arms, and running with a determined shout, splashed them into the stream. The water was cold, and she shouted with surprise, even as the icy sensations invigorated every nerve ending in her body and drew her to Nicholai's heat. He splashed along the glossy stones, nearly slipping twice, until he hopped over a fallen tree trunk and dunked them head to toe into a sweet, still pond.

The water was warmer here and the minute they emerged from beneath the surface and pulled in great gulps of air, Nicholai's mouth clashed over hers. He grabbed her waist and lifted her high, sucking the glistening water from her breasts in great, thirsty gulps. Danielle cried out, whether in the vision or in real time, she had no idea. The sensations were exquisite—wild, and yet concentrated. Not just the physical delight pleased her, but the complete freedom of surrendering her body to a man she trusted and loved with all her soul.

She didn't dare stay in the vision. She didn't dare allow herself to experience the sensual decadence of this encounter, did she? She wasn't this woman. She couldn't have been. And yet, how else would she be seeing the scene with such vivid clarity? It wasn't like watching a movie. She couldn't see herself. She likened the experience more to watching a videotape she'd shot from her own camera. Except instead of just seeing, she was hearing, feeling, wanting, as well.

"I missed you," Nicholai growled, his lips nipping and suckling along her neck and shoulder. "Never leave me again."

"I won't have to. The marriage pact my father made for me is broken. I'm free to be your wife, my love."

Danielle nearly shouted when Nicholai pushed her away and dived beneath the water. She glanced around, confused, unable to see anything in the inky pond. In an instant, Nicholai emerged like a proud, untamed sea creature, breaching the water with a whoop of total joy.

She heard herself laugh, felt her limbs ache as she swam to catch up. He grabbed her, spun her in the water, kissed her face from brow to chin and whispered in another language about how he adored her, how he'd make her the happiest woman alive.

And Danielle understood every word. Not only that, but the power of his promise melted her insides so that she no longer felt the cold of the night or the wind on her sodden flesh. She knew nothing more than intense desire that only he could fill.

She tugged him toward the shore, then crawled onto

the grass with him right behind her. He spooned her body with his from behind, and with one free hand, plucked at her nipples until her body rippled with need.

His cock teased the sweet folds between her legs and she couldn't help but spread her knees to give him access. How often had she succumbed to Nicholai's seductive charms, even when she was betrothed to another man? He'd been irresistible, gentle. Discreet. Every woman in the caravan wanted Nicholai in her bed, yet he'd waited for her. No one beyond the two of them knew that they'd made love before they could be bound by the spirits of their ancestors into a marriage for life.

He rubbed the tip of his sex against hers. "You want me like this?"

She reached beneath her belly and through her legs, guiding him inside her, kneeling on the ground, wet with water and pure undeniable lust. "I want you every way I can have you."

He curved over her, his muscled stomach and chest gliding over her back, his balls gently slapping her thighs. He arched into her, hard and deep, pressing toward pleasure with an intensity that made her gasp. A rhythm snagged them instantly, hot with want, slick with need. Her flesh ached for his and when he shifted his balance so he could squeeze her nipples, she screamed out his name.

Climax came swiftly for both of them. They weren't shy about crying into the night. The sounds mingled with the wind and the forest, reverberating with a natural music that felt so right. Never in her life had Danielle heard anything more unbridled, more innately free.

After a moment of remembering how to breathe, their laughter filled the air as his weight pressed her to the grassy shore. She rolled over beneath him and in one split second, Danielle knew she couldn't stay any longer.

She pressed her eyes closed and concentrated. With a yank not unlike someone trying to pull her arms from the sockets, she bolted into the here and now.

She dropped the bottle. It fell, unbroken, onto the rug. Danielle wanted nothing more than to run, to escape, but she couldn't move. Her muscles simply wouldn't obey the commands shouted from her brain.

Nick reached beneath the table, retrieved the bottle and replaced it in the box. This time, he closed the case and secured the latch. Then, without looking her in the eyes, without saying a single word, he stood and lifted her into his arms. She couldn't speak, couldn't protest. She was frozen, both by her physical reaction to the magic and from the utter absoluteness of the love she'd once shared for a man she felt sure she'd never known.

He laid her on his bed, which she realized was tucked behind a tall privacy screen. He touched her only to remove her boots, then covered her with a blanket that instantly brought warmth to her icy veins.

"Sleep now, Danielle. I'll be downstairs in the workshop if you need me."

She opened her mouth to speak, but what could she say? Her experience had been physically and emotionally overwhelming. The lovemaking she'd lived through in the dream had been amazing—hot, passionate, wild…and yet, brimming with the kind of love that happens only once in a lifetime. If then.

With a shiver, she grabbed the edge of the blanket, pulled it to her chin and rolled into a ball on his bed. She couldn't process all that had happened tonight. She couldn't think. She could only sleep—and hope to God, she didn't dream.

8

NICHOLAI FOUND HIMSELF drawn to the street. After one last longing glance at the upstairs loft where Danielle still slept, he abandoned the carving he'd been working on since midnight and slipped outside into the oppressive Chicago sunshine. He locked the door, but kept the deadbolt free so she could leave if she woke up and wished to go. He doubted she'd awake in the next hour, but if she did, he knew where to find her.

Neither one of them could escape what they'd started last night.

August dawned with a heavy heat, kindled and stoked by the miles of concrete and asphalt and glass all around them. Despite the cloying warmth, Nicholai shoved his hands in his pockets and proceeded to walk with steady, measured steps, trying not to think about what he would say to Danielle once she woke up. What could he say? *I loved you when you were Sofia. I thought I'd love you instantly now, but I just realized I don't know enough about you?*

Countless times during the night, he'd checked on her. She hadn't moved as much as a muscle. Curled in a ball, breathing steadily, unhindered by nightmares or dreams, she slept. The experience had exhausted her. He guessed she wouldn't wake for at least another few hours. He, too, had suffered draining effects—but nowhere near what she'd gone through. After all, he'd chosen the memory she would see.

He'd told her last night that he couldn't have drawn out the memory if she hadn't had it stored somewhere in her subconscious, but now he wasn't so sure. He'd followed Viktor's instructions to the letter. He'd touched the bottle first this time, to transfer the memory he'd relived in his own mind a hundred times in the past year. His memory was only supposed to trigger hers, but what if it had gone farther?

He'd known how that sultry night by the pond would progress and he'd chosen that snippet precisely because of how intense that coupling had been. As many times as he and Sofia had made love both before and after they'd married, that one time after she'd been freed of her bonds of betrothal had been unforgettable.

For the first time, they'd been free to love each other completely, and they'd done so with a raw, animalistic force. The teasing and flirtations they'd shared for months had been stripped away to the most basic carnal needs. And yet, the sex had revitalized their love. From that moment on, they'd kept no secrets, played no games. They'd loved openly and honestly. And he'd never forgotten.

But she had.

He didn't fool himself. Danielle had witnessed the scene he'd chosen, but probably only because of the magic, not because the bottle had pulled the scene from her own experience. Viktor had been clear—the magic would drain her, weaken her—unless the memory came from her own trove of life knowledge. And she'd been weakened to the point of exhaustion.

He'd gone too far, and yet, he couldn't help but speculate about what might happen if he pushed harder. His time was running out. When he returned to the loft, he had to say the right thing, or she'd disappear from his life for good. He didn't know much for certain, but he believed he had one more shot to convince Danielle of the truth. If it was the truth. Damn, but he was no longer so sure.

And he had to be. There could be no more secrets, no more scheming, no more wasted time. To push her beyond the boundaries of reality, he had to seduce her again. In the present, not the past.

And to do that, he had to find out more about the real Danielle Stone, far beyond the information in the magazine article or the observations of a casual friend in a coffee shop. Last night over pizza, he'd finally gotten a true glimpse of the woman who'd turned her life around after years of neglect and drug abuse. He needed to know more about what drove her, what comforted her. What were her passions? Her needs? Her fears?

How had she survived her years on the streets?

That question had driven him out of the warehouse more than any other. He crossed the intersection at Racine and West 18th, walking without direction, knowing precisely where he'd end up. He looked down as he walked, angered by the stains and cracks in the concrete—the trappings of modern life slowly crumbling beneath his feet. Nothing lasted. Nothing.

Not even love?

The moment the terrain beneath his boots shifted from hard to soft, the weight in his chest lightened. He marched over the grass, ignoring the sparse thinness and brown tinge on the blades. To either side, scraggly oaks struggled to breathe in the choked city air. The El train rattled just a few blocks away and bass notes from a nearby boom box pounded against his ears. Chicago had some of the most beautiful city parks in the state, including nearby Dvorak, but this nameless gathering spot wasn't one of them. It was, however, close to Nicholai's warehouse and one continually peopled with kids who'd run away from home.

All night long, he'd thought of nothing else but what Danielle's life had been like before her brother rescued her and swept her away to Paris to heal. He understood how Sofia's residual spirit might have led her to seek out freedom from the constraints of her life with her uncaring parents, but he'd never imagined that Danielle had never been loved by the family who'd brought her into the world. Knowing what he did about her brother, Danielle's past of violence, terror and darkness seemed unbelievable. Though she hadn't given him many details about her life on the streets, he hadn't needed them. He'd watched the runaways. As a gypsy, he'd once known the same hunger, the same desperation to move and connect to new places in the world. But also because he'd been a gypsy, raised to face such realities with no illusions or romanticism, he'd never felt lost or trapped.

He couldn't say the same for the quartet of dirty kids lounging on a park bench half-defaced by graffiti, the other half ruined by rotting wood and chipped concrete. He could hardly tell which were the girls and which were the boys. All had shaved their heads. The odor of cheap cigarettes reeked around them, heavy like the chains dripping from their pockets and the piercings marring otherwise attractive faces. Nicholai circled them on the gravel path, knowing he couldn't say anything to them. He suspected that if he made a wrong move, he could find himself at the other end of a razor-sharp shank. He had no desire to have to defend himself against four kids whose narcotics might lend them a viciousness they didn't normally possess.

Still, he wanted to speak to them. Why, he wasn't sure.

"Nicholai?"

He spun around. Jeta stood beside him, stooped, but vital, holding a small basket covered with a cloth.

"Jeta? What are you doing here?"

"Looking for you. I have news."

Her words were emotionless, but weighted with import. He rarely questioned how the old woman could find him so easily, no matter where he'd gone. Jeta did not reveal her secrets.

"What news?"

She took his arm and led him away from the four runaways, who hadn't seemed to notice their proximity, or else, they simply hadn't cared. When his grandmother reached a second bench, similarly decayed and sitting on a plot of earth stinking of stale beer and urine, he helped her sit, then took the place beside her.

She glanced at the morning sun, hazy in a cloudless sky. The lines on her face seemed more like gouges today, deepened by worry.

"Is it Alexis?" he asked.

For the most part, Jeta cared about only two people—him and his cousin. And since he knew he was essentially fine, he suspected the same wasn't true for Alexis.

Jeta pursed her lips, fiddled with the cloth on the basket, then turned and eyed him squarely.

"I spoke with her this morning. She's seen you, Nicholai. You and this Danielle Stone."

Nicholai's heart stopped, then rushed to make up for the missed beat. His cousin, Alexis, had the Sight. When they were traveling with the caravan, she'd brought in many coins telling fortunes. But as she sat in the tent behind her ball of crystal, she'd rarely used her real talent. She'd simply regaled the *gaujo* with mystical stories and predictions borne of her own imagination.

For her own people, however, Alexis provided true guidance. She'd predicted births, illness, famine and feast. She'd been the one to tell Sofia that she was destined to marry Nicholai, not the man her father had promised her to.

But since their return from the afterlife, Alexis hadn't experienced a single vision. Jeta and Nicholai suspected the shift from the old world to the new had been too much for Alexis's gentle soul, but with each passing day, she'd grown more confident, more acclimated to her new life. That she'd finally experienced her gift again was cause for great joy—and also great fear.

The look on Jeta's face was grave. Whatever Alexis had seen hadn't been good.

"What did she see?"

Jeta licked her wizened lips, then reached out and grabbed Nicholai's hands, as if to inject him with her calming strength.

"She saw Milosh, Nicholai."

"That's it? So what?" he scoffed. Milosh had been the man betrothed to his Sofia all those years ago—a man long dead. A year after their broken engagement and Nicholai's subsequent marriage to Sofia, Milosh had come to join their clan and had wed one of Sofia's cousins in conciliation. Though Nicholai had never argued with the man, never so much as exchanged a cross word, the tension between them had always sailed on a dangerous undercurrent of anger and jealousy. He'd often wondered, without proof, if Milosh had been somehow responsible for Sofia's disappearance.

He hadn't thought about the man for a century. He'd focused his attention only on his love for Sofia, his quest to get her back. He couldn't let Milosh's negative energy derail him now.

"Milosh died many years ago," he concluded.

Jeta pulled his hands toward her, forcing his face closer to hers. "So did you. So did I. So did Sofia. Death is not an indestructible warrior, Nicholai. Alexis knows what she speaks of. Her visions are true. Milosh is back and according to your cousin, he is near."

DANIELLE AWOKE with the force of a drowning woman breaking the surface for the final time. With a gasp, she pulled air into her lungs. Her eyes flew open wide, but she was instantly blinded by sunlight. Grasping the sheets in fisted hands, Danielle fought sleep, which threatened to drag her back into unconsciousness.

Where was she? She squinted, forced herself to make sense of her surroundings. She calmed when she realized she was still in Nick's loft and though she was still exhausted, her strength had returned.

"Oh, God. Danielle! Are you all right?"

Danielle shook her head and battled with her leaded eyelids until she could finally see.

"Margo?"

Her friend dashed forward. Dressed in hip-hugging jeans and a halter-style tank top, her hair a saucy collection of curls, Margo's stylishly carefree look contrasted with her serious expression. Danielle realized she'd never really seen Margo out of her coffee shop uniform and hadn't realized how lithe and feminine she was.

"Geez, Danielle. I've been trying to wake you up for fifteen minutes," Margo said, clearly more worried than annoyed. "What happened to you? Are you okay? Do you need a doctor?"

Danielle groaned and allowed herself to fall back into the bed, though she didn't dare shut her eyes. "Yeah, a psychiatrist, maybe."

Danielle didn't make the joke lightly. Not when she had so much evidence to support the contention that she was losing her mind. And this time, without the mind-numbing accompaniment of drugs. Life wasn't fair.

She remembered the events of the night before with perfect clarity. The bottle. The vision by the pond. The pleasurable pain of hard and heavy sex. The gut-

wrenching realization of true and timeless love. How
she'd slept without replaying the powerful scene in her
mind over and over shocked her. But mercifully, she
hadn't dreamed last night. In fact, though a quick
glance at her watch told her she'd slept for nearly ten
hours, she felt like she'd dozed for only five minutes.
Her stomach churned and her muscles ached. She
craved another ten hours of sleep, or else a scalding
hot shower and a stiff cup of Margo's espresso.

Margo slipped onto the edge of the bed. "What are
you doing here anyway? No one could find you. You
don't have your cell phone on."

Danielle sat up against the pillows, searching
through squinted eyes for her bag. She saw it on the
floor beside the coffee table. The wooden box that contained the perfume bottle still sat in the center, decep-
tively lifeless.

She gestured toward the bag, causing Margo to in-
terpret her move as a request to retrieve the oversized
purse. With a dry mouth, she thanked Margo and dug
inside. She found her cell phone, but it had no power.

"I guess I didn't recharge it yesterday," she spec-
ulated. "How did you find me?"

Margo shrugged. "A little deductive reasoning. You
and this carpenter guy seemed pretty taken with each
other yesterday in the store, so I just talked to one of
the workmen who'd helped with the furniture delivery
and he gave me this address." She shook her thumb
toward the front entrance. "I knocked and rang the
buzzer, but there wasn't an answer. I thought maybe
he was working and couldn't hear me. I jimmied the
lock. I hope you don't mind."

Danielle tossed her powerless cell phone back into her bag, her hackles raised by Margo's story. Breaking and entering didn't seem like her style, but when she stared into her friend's wide eyes, she saw nothing but sincerity and concern. Danielle had bent a few laws in her past when she'd felt the end justified the means. Who was she to judge?

"Okay, you've answered how you found me. Next question is why?"

Margo's gaze widened and she grabbed Danielle's hands. "Oh, my God! Cecily Divine came into the coffee shop this morning with one of your foremen. There's been an accident at the job site and no one could get in touch with you. They tried to find Micki, but she was in class and they'd decided they would contact your brother instead. I knew you wouldn't like that, seeing as you're always saying you don't want him to have to rescue you and everything all the time, so I told them to give me an hour to look for you myself."

Margo dug into her pocket and retrieved her own cell phone. "Here, call Cecily right away. Your brother would be so worried if he found out you were missing!"

Danielle dialed quickly. Worried wasn't the word for the emotions Bas would experience if Danielle disappeared, even for one night. And the last thing she needed right now was her brother riding to her rescue yet again, especially when she didn't need help.

Her phone call with Cecily did not ease her nerves. While she zipped on her boots and hunted through the huge warehouse for a bathroom, she learned that an entire wall of scaffolding had fallen during the night. Light fixtures left on the temporary structure for installation had been ruined, and they suspected that once the steel and wooden railings were removed, the tile floor, original to the building, would be damaged beyond repair.

The construction site was in an uproar and where was she? Brushing her teeth with her finger in a stranger's bathroom, that's where.

"I'll be right there, Cecily. Give me twenty minutes. Don't call Sebastian. I'll contact him myself as soon as I assess the damage. I'll alert the insurance agent on my way in."

She disconnected the call and nearly rammed into Margo, who stood at the bottom of the stairs leading from Nick's loft, Danielle's bag in her hand.

Danielle handed her the cell phone. "Thanks, Margo." She took the bag and glanced inside. Margo hadn't put the wooden box back into her bag and for an instant, Danielle wondered if she should go back upstairs and retrieve it. The connection that had been so irresistible between her and the bottle yesterday now appeared more tenuous. Common sense insisted that the bottle might have brought her pleasure, but it wouldn't provide even a dash of peace of mind. Best to leave it behind, at least for now.

"I need to get to the construction site. Did you drive?"

Margo shook her head. "I took a cab. We can call for another one on the way out."

"There's no need," Nick said, appearing from around a collection of shelves.

The minute his eyes met hers, Danielle experienced a renewed wash of weakness. The pit of her stomach had never felt so empty and while she was sure she'd felt this light-headed before, she hadn't for a very long time.

"Nick," she said. "Margo came to find me. There's been an accident at the construction site."

The suspicious, guarded look on his face disappeared, replaced with one of complete concern. "Was anyone hurt?"

Danielle shook her head. "No, it happened during the night. But construction could be seriously set back. I need to get over there to assess the damage."

He nodded. "I'll drive you. Let me grab my keys."

After Nick disappeared upstairs, Danielle noticed that Margo was gazing around the warehouse, her eyes looking anywhere but at Nick and Danielle.

"What's wrong?" she asked.

Margo shrugged. "Just worried about your work. And about you. You look a little, I don't know, freaked out."

Danielle laughed and ran her hand through her hair. Thank God she'd cut it short. Made jumping out of bed and dashing out the door a whole lot less traumatic, especially to the rest of the world. She plopped her bag onto a nearby workbench and fished inside for some gum or heavy-duty mints to waylay her morning breath.

Margo appeared at her side, a small tin of mints extended toward her.

"How'd you know I was looking for mints?"

Margo giggled and glanced toward Nick's loft.

"You aren't the first woman to stay at a guy's place completely unprepared, you know."

Danielle nodded and accepted the candy. Margo would have been shocked to learn how completely unprepared Danielle had truly been. Then again, exactly how do you prepare yourself for learning that you might be the reincarnated lover of a mysterious gypsy craftsman?

She thought about the perfume bottle, and realized she could finally part with it. The connection between her and the purported magic still tingled beneath her skin, but it had accomplished its task. She'd witnessed the scene from her past. Now she needed a few clear moments to make sense of what she'd experienced.

Nick appeared a second later and locked the building behind them before directing them toward his truck. They squeezed into the cab, Danielle in the center, while Margo and Nick chatted about traffic and coffee, both of them obviously trying to keep her mind off the disaster she would face once they arrived at Pillow Talk.

Danielle found the fifteen-minute drive slightly surreal. Behind her, she'd left a mystical piece of what might be her past life, a possible key to the soul-searching questions that had plagued her since childhood. Who was she? Why did she always feel so lost? When would she finally find someone or something to connect to? In front of her, her future success might lay in ruins. She'd had the project on time and under budget from the first day. Yes, the overall plan provided for unavoidable setbacks, but she'd been sailing so smoothly up until now, she'd thought she was free and clear.

She should have known better.

"Are you going to call your brother?" Margo asked, finally breaking the silence.

Danielle glanced surreptitiously at Nick. What would Sebastian think about her new friend? Would Nick Davis, aka Nicholai Vaux—a rogue gypsy who believed she possessed the spirit of his dead lover—qualify as a wise choice?

She groaned. "Whatever mess awaits me, I'll handle it."

She just wished she could say the same about the mess she'd left behind.

9

A CROWD OF two dozen workers loitered outside the building on the steps, drinking coffee, smoking cigarettes and shaking their heads, undoubtedly discussing how fatal the accident would have been if anyone had been on the scaffolding when it tumbled to the ground. A brownish-gray haze of dust and smoke lingered in the air, which smelled of concrete and metal. Danielle's primary foreman, a brawny redheaded Irishman named Doyle, stood like a sentinel just inside the doorway, his arms crossed and his expression dire. He moved aside only when Danielle jogged up the steps, darting around workers without a single word.

The destruction shocked even Nicholai.

Yesterday, the scaffolding had created a steady, crisscross matrix of steel and wood across the entire west wall of the building, two stories high and nearly ninety feet in length. Workers had swarmed over the structure like bees on honeycomb, replacing out-of-code wiring, refurbishing pipes, repairing years of neglect and damage to the concrete wall by applying sealant, paint and tile, and masking the upgrades so that, after the restaurant opened, not a single patron would notice the painstaking work. Nicholai guessed that when he'd been in the building yesterday, no less than ten workmen had traversed the framework at one time, and ten more had crossed under, around and beside it on their way to other tasks in the building. No doubt, if the scaffolding had given way during the day, the body count would be nothing short of tragic.

"How did this happen?" Danielle asked, her voice choked either from the air or from the emotions of the destruction.

Doyle shook his head, his jaw tight. "No word yet. I paged the engineers." With a nod, he indicated two men picking through the rubble wearing hard hats and thick leather gloves. "They're still looking things over."

"Has OSHA been called?"

"Cecily Divine came by this morning just after we discovered the accident. She's filing a report from her office, but since no one was in the building when this happened, they aren't rushing over until after the engineers work up their theories. But we're shut down, Ms. Stone. No way is this place going to be fit for work anytime soon."

Danielle grunted and hitched her hands on her hips. "We'll see about that. Can I get to my office?"

Doyle shook his head. "Not in those shoes. What do you need?"

"My hard hat and my steel-toed boots. I want to check out the damage for myself."

Doyle nodded and marched around the debris to fetch her things. Nicholai sidestepped a few inches to stand directly beside her. He watched her scan the destruction with slow precision and observed how keenly she listened to the chatter of the two engineers as they pored over the destruction with careful consideration. All of the fear and uncertainty he'd witnessed in her eyes the night before had disappeared. Facing hard truths in her personal life was obviously harder for her than confronting the possibility of failure in business.

Not that Nicholai thought for one minute that she'd fail. Or even that she thought she'd fail. He could practically see the gears in her brain churning and clicking, working out a solution to the destruction and delays the project now faced. Would his Sofia have reacted similarly? The truth was, he'd never know. Sofia hadn't been one to take on responsibilities that affected anyone but the two of them. For the two years of their marriage, they'd practically existed on a remote island, two lovers stranded by a mad and constant passion. They'd never thought about the future. They'd lived only in the moment, which had made the instance of her disappearance all the more catastrophic.

Doyle soon returned with Danielle's things and just after she finished changing her shoes and securing her hard hat, one of the engineers reached her.

"Ms. Stone, you need to see this," he said.

Nicholai resisted the urge to grab her arm when she instantly lunged forward. Instead, he stepped slightly into her path, delaying her movement. "Is it safe?"

The man nodded. "The scaffolding is completely on the floor and no glass or debris can penetrate those boots. Just watch your step."

Danielle spared Nick an amused though slightly annoyed glance, then followed the engineer through the maze of twisted steel and splintered wood. Nicholai borrowed a hard hat from one of the workmen outside, then hopped across to where Danielle, Doyle and the engineer knelt in a corner beside an emergency exit.

"Right here." The inspector gestured toward a melted and twisted steel pole, jagged, sharp and blackened.

Danielle leaned forward. "Blowtorch?"

The inspector nodded. "No doubt."

Doyle cursed. "I supervised the construction of that scaffolding myself. One little blowtorch could not have brought the structure down."

The engineer glanced up at his partner, who joined them with a strange device in his hand. Though now a semiflat charred twist of metal, Nicholai recognized the remnants of another blowtorch, this one attached to a makeshift stand.

"Several blowtorches, lit at precisely the same time on the most crucial points of the structure could do this," the second engineer informed them. "Not an easy task, but obviously, it could be done—if someone wanted to tear your scaffolding down fast enough."

"So this wasn't an accident," Nicholai asked.

Both the engineers and Doyle shook their heads.

"Sabotage?" Danielle said, her voice a blend of a disbelieving gasp and a furious growl.

The engineer stood, removed his gloves. "That's my guess. Sabotage or some kids out looking for kicks. I mean, the damage could have been a hell of a lot worse. We got off lucky. No one was hurt and the structure of the building hasn't been affected, though I imagine the floor tiles underneath this mess have been shattered beyond repair. Still, if someone did do this to try to shut you down, you need to call the police."

Danielle stood, blowing out a frustrated breath. "What about cleanup? When can we start?"

The engineers exchanged glances. "Not until after the police have investigated, which will likely take the rest of the day. If you're lucky, you can complete all the cleanup by tomorrow or the next day. Then we can better assess the damage. We'll have to rebuild the scaffolding, of course, and replace the light fixtures and broken tools. We'll lose, at my estimate, about a week."

She nodded quietly, thanked the engineers for their quick response and then directed Doyle to dismiss the men for the day while she dialed the police. At that moment, Nicholai wished he possessed some of Aloda's talent for foretelling the future. Perhaps through her Sight, she could identify whoever had targeted Danielle's project for destruction. Maybe he'd know then how to help her, beyond standing there like a statue.

Still, Danielle didn't seem to mind his presence or else she would have asked him to leave. He was a contractor with fifteen more beds to build—he wasn't needed here. And yet, when the police arrived thirty minutes later, she nodded for him to join her so they could ask her the standard questions. He didn't say a word or volunteer one helpful suggestion or piece of information, and yet, when she glanced at him with a weary smile, his pride surged. She needed him near. Whether the phenomenon resulted from the bottle's magic, he didn't know and didn't care. He just wanted to stay.

An hour later, the case detective called in crime investigators from the fire department, whose specialized knowledge confirmed the theory that ten blowtorches— nine set on stands—had been placed at various joints and ignited. Under the blue-hot heat, the scaffolding bars had melted and the structure, heavy with its own weight, had crumbled onto itself. The tenth torch, lit only a few feet from the emergency exit, was likely held by the saboteur himself, with the door to the outside a perfect, quick getaway.

The security guard Danielle had hired to watch the building at night was nowhere to be found. Suspecting foul play, the police made an exhaustive search of the building and came up empty. At noon, the guard was finally located having lunch at his favorite sports bar. He'd come down to the site immediately, claiming that he'd received a phone message, reportedly from Doyle, telling him to take the night off because the crews were working late.

Which, of course, had been a lie.

"I didn't call him, Ms. Stone," Doyle insisted after the guard had left, his statement in the hands of the police.

Danielle patted the brawny man on the shoulder. "I believe you, Doyle. Anyone could have called him and said it was you."

"I suppose. But I'm told I have an accent. How would an anonymous caller know that?"

Danielle glanced at the detective, who seemed too engrossed in his notes to respond. "I'll bet they didn't even try, Doyle. The man obviously wanted to take the night off. Who wouldn't?"

Doyle nodded curtly and stalked away, determinedly

watching as much of the police investigation as possible. Adjusters from the insurance company had arrived and were snapping pictures and assessing the cost of repair and replacement. That was one bill Nicholai wouldn't want to foot.

"Do you believe Doyle?" Nicholai asked once they were out of earshot. His impression of Doyle was that the foreman was honest, hard working and would never betray his employer, but what did Nicholai truly know about these matters? He was, after all, new to this century. Morals and honor weren't quite as valued as they'd been in his distant past.

Danielle turned into her office and motioned him inside. Despite her long hours of hard sleep, she looked utterly exhausted. The skin beneath her eyes was bruised dark blue and the whites around her irises were streaked with red. A smudge of dirt marred her pale cheek, which she worsened when she swiped at it with her gloves.

"Yeah, I believe him. Doyle's been with the project from the beginning. Since I'm so inexperienced, Bas enticed him to work for us with a very generous offer. He's a top commercial renovation contractor and his reputation means everything to him. I don't think he'd be bribed easily."

Nicholai rolled his neck, unnerved by the guilt of knowing that some of her fatigue had been his doing. He'd known the magic might have an adverse effect on her, but never had he suspected the experience would wipe her out so completely. Before he dealt with the question of whether or not he'd employ the magic again, he spied a coffeemaker in the corner of her of-

fice. He briefly considered inviting her to the coffeehouse across the street for a break, but he didn't want
to run into Margo. The waitress hadn't appreciated not
being allowed inside the building when they'd first arrived and had stalked back to her place of business in
quite a foul mood.

He crossed the room and popped the top off a jug
of bottled water to fill the carafe. "Do you think this
is competitors again, like the fake inspector?" he
asked.

"Who else?" She plopped down onto her chair and
tore off her gloves, which she threw angrily at the window that provided a view of the destruction. "But it
doesn't make sense. This is the restaurant business, not
a war between nations. This project isn't even contro-
versial for the neighborhood. In fact, it's really popular,
what with the new movie theater a half block away and
the coffeehouse and the art galleries nearby. A big,
popular restaurant here is good for business and prop-
erty values."

After pouring the grounds into the filter and pressing
the button for the coffee to brew, he joined her at her
desk. He leaned on the corner nearest her, wanting to
wrap his arms around her and order her to relax. He
figured commands wouldn't go very far with her, so he
concentrated instead on helping solve her dilemma.

"What about personal vendettas?" he asked. "Anyone out there who would like to see you fail?"

Nicholai didn't like that his mind automatically
moved in that direction, but he'd been raised in a culture where revenge against some real or imagined

slight could cost a man both his livelihood and his life. It had cost him his, back in that Georgia field.

"I don't know anyone here," she insisted. "I mean, yeah, I pissed off a few drug and porno dealers during my time on the street, but that was over a year ago. Most of those losers wouldn't even know where to find me, much less care about what I'm doing now. And if it was aimed personally at me, wouldn't there be some sort of note? Some version of na-na-na-na-boo-boo that can't be easily traced?"

Nicholai chuckled. "Cowards take revenge in silence."

Danielle leaned forward on her desk, cradling her head in her hands. "There are so many people involved in this project, any one of them could be a target for revenge. The contractors, the investors. My brother. The Divines. Who knows?" She lifted her head, her eyes wide. "Oh, God. I have to call Bas."

The inevitable discussion with her brother was delayed by a knock on the door from the lead detective. He'd finished interviewing the workers who'd first discovered the accident, along with several adjacent business owners, and he wanted to fill Danielle in. Apparently, no one had reported seeing anything unusual, though several tenants living in the building next door had called 911 to report the sound of a crash at around four o'clock in the morning. Police had responded, but found the building secure, so they'd moved on.

Once the detective had completed a rundown of his investigation, he asked Nicholai to leave so he could interview Danielle one more time.

He hoped she wanted him to stay.

She didn't.

"I'd like to go into the VIP room," he said before leaving. "To check on the…furniture."

Her cheeks, pale since she'd awoken this morning, now flushed with a subtle pink. "Of course. Doyle has the key."

Nicholai grinned only after he'd turned toward the door. Hopefully, her blush meant that thinking about the bed he'd created aroused her. Last night's memory had been emotionally draining, he admitted, but he'd watched her titillation with utter captivation. The way her breath had become shallow, her lips moist. The way her nipples had peaked and hardened beneath her blouse. The way she'd squeezed her thighs tightly together and gasped for breath before she'd dropped the bottle into his hands. She'd experienced firsthand the intense physical attraction he'd shared with his wife, and he intended to share the same with Danielle. Very, very soon.

The VIP room was a small, intimate dining area on the other side of the main hall. Available only to the highest paying customers, the room would accommodate high-profile guests like movie stars and sports celebrities, both of which were in large supply in Chicago. In the VIP room, they would enjoy impeccable service and guaranteed privacy. Danielle had explained the concept to him with total innocence in her eyes, but Nicholai figured that all manner of intimate acts would occur on the bed he'd created for that room.

A brilliant concept, in his opinion.

Doyle provided a passkey, and they were both relieved to find the bed untouched by the vandal who'd attacked the scaffolding. The comforter looked slightly rumpled, as if someone had used the private space to lie down, or perhaps, the Divines had tried out the comfort of their unique serving "table" during the meeting yesterday afternoon.

The thought of making love to Danielle on that bed filled his body and soul with insatiable desire. Never had he and Sofia made love on a bed so luxurious or extravagant. Their tiny mattress in his *vardo* had provided all the comfort and luxury they'd needed, which hadn't been much.

For the first time, Nicholai realized that since he'd started spending time with Danielle, the differences between her and Sofia had become more marked, more distinct. At the heart, they both possessed the same free spirit, the same sensual soul, but where Sofia had loved life openly, Danielle moved with caution. Sofia possessed a simplistic outlook on the world and her place in it, but Danielle's life had a complexity that fascinated him. He feared that the more he learned about Danielle Stone, the less he would see the remnants of his lost love.

But was this a bad thing?

"I'm going to get back and see if Ms. Stone needs me for anything more," Doyle said, tossing Nicholai the keys. "Lock up after you check things out."

Nicholai did his inspection quickly, but carefully. Apparently, no one had thought to come into this room, though he made sure the doors leading to the VIP suite from the private bathrooms and the kitchen were bolted and secure. Satisfied, Nicholai turned to leave when he noticed an odd change on the wall.

Yesterday, when he'd delivered and assembled the bed, the suite had been painted in a solitary oyster-shell color with no decoration or definition. Now, a rainbow of hues were splashed on the walls—a pale blue, a light green, a pink reminiscent of the inside of a shell. The shapes were blotchlike, but painted with obvious control. Not being an artist, Nicholai had no idea what the purpose was, but he was still intrigued. The forms were innately sensual, compelling. He wondered about the artist and what exactly was planned for this room.

By the time he returned to Danielle's office, the interview with the officer was over. The inspectors and investigators were gone and after receiving permission from his boss, Doyle had left for his own office in a trailer out back to order the materials needed for the repairs.

Danielle sat behind her desk, drumming her fingers on the handset of her phone, her eyes flashing with an emotion he couldn't identify.

"You called your brother?" Nicholai asked.

She nodded, her lips pursed. "He's in Taipei. The police will interview him later by phone."

Nick closed the door behind him, surprised by the news. "He's not coming?"

Her eyes widened and her head shook with disbelief. "Nope. Says I can handle it."

Nicholai's stomach churned. For a man with a hell of a lot of money, Sebastian Stone obviously had no sense. Whoever had knocked down the scaffolding clearly had an agenda. Even vandals could strike again, and this time, Danielle and her crew might not be so lucky. Besides, Nicholai realized that Danielle's success with the restaurant represented a goal more important than fiscal achievement. She'd been trying to change her life. If she failed, she could return to the vortex of loss and fear that had sucked her down before.

"Doesn't he think you might be in danger?"

Danielle speared him with a disbelieving glare. "Danger? What are you talking about? Someone sabotaged my project, yes, but there is no evidence that I was targeted personally. The police suspect vandals. The blowtorches that were used were ours, stolen from a storage area behind the kitchen."

"Vandals? What about the security guard?" he pressed. "He was obviously kept off the job for a reason."

She blew out a frustrated breath. "Was he? Was he even telling the truth? Maybe he had a hot date and just cut out of work and made up the story about Doyle calling him and giving him the night off. Anyway, I have a new security firm coming tonight and I'm thinking of staying here myself, just in case."

That was the final straw. Nicholai stalked forward and slammed his hand down on his desk. "You will do no such thing. It is too dangerous."

Fire gleamed in her eyes, no doubt matching his own fiery gaze. She braced her hands on her desk and slowly pushed herself to her feet. She leaned forward, her voice growling through clenched teeth. "Tell me you just didn't issue an order to me."

Nicholai could not back down. His brain spun back to his conversation this morning with Jeta, about Alexis and her vision of the return of Milosh. Though Nicholai had no proof that the man Sofia had been engaged to had in any way been responsible for her disappearance, he did know that Milosh had been the ringleader behind the suspicions that had been thrown at Nicholai. That Nicholai had killed Sofia. That Nicholai had thrown his beloved wife off the cliff where they'd found her scarf because he'd caught her staring at another man. And of course, that man had been Milosh.

Because of the poisonous accusations, Nicholai, Jeta and Alexis had had to leave the clan. They'd traveled to America, only to be murdered soon after when Alexis's visions had frightened the wrong family. Though Nicholai wasn't a bitter man, he couldn't deny that curses and *wafdo bak*—bad luck—had haunted him and his family whenever Milosh had played a role in their lives. If he was back, had the bad luck extended to Danielle as well? And if the soul of Milosh was near, would he actually try to hurt the person who possessed the spirit of the woman he'd once loved and lost?

But Nicholai wasn't a stupid man. He leveled his tone and unclenched his fists before he spoke to Danielle again.

"Bad word choice. Danielle, you mean a great deal to me. I don't want to see you hurt."

She laughed, but the sound lacked all lightness or humor. "*I* mean a great deal to you? Me, Danielle Stone, the poor little rich girl from Michigan, the street kid who abused her body with drugs and sex? The recovering addict who is trying with all her heart and soul to make a new life for herself? That woman means a lot to you? Or do you simply care about this mysterious woman you think I am? This woman you loved in another lifetime, if any of that is true and not some powerful suggestion you've planted into my mind.''

Nicholai took a deep breath, then spoke through clenched teeth. ''Her name was Sofia.''

The admission stopped her rant, but didn't assuage the anger in her eyes.

He pushed further. ''She was murdered.''

She swallowed. ''I don't want to hear this.''

''Why not? Afraid you might remember who pushed you off the cliff one hundred years ago? Afraid you might realize that your murderer was someone you trusted never to harm you?''

Her eyes widened, her voice a shocked whisper. ''You?''

Bile burbled up the back of his throat. ''I couldn't prove my innocence then any more than you can prove that you are not in danger now. Can't you for once simply trust me?''

He shouldn't have snapped, but he had his limits. The accusations still rubbed him raw. Unfortunately, confronting Danielle's anger with more anger pushed her too far—especially when he'd spoken to her as if she were Sofia, instead of Danielle. She kicked her chair out of her way, then stalked to the door, tearing it open with such force, Nicholai expected the hinges to come free.

They didn't. She didn't say another word, but stood there with her intention clear.

She wanted him to leave.

He took a deep, calming breath, then reached out to her with an open palm. ''I'm sorry. I never found out exactly how Sofia died, or who was responsible, but

I've always known it was a man she trusted. You're surrounded by people you don't know. How can I know you are safe?"

Her eyes were narrow slits. "My safety is not your concern. I'm not Sofia."

His breath hitched. She couldn't deny what she'd seen, not when he'd come this far. "You know what you saw last night was real."

She spat out a curse. "I know no such thing. What I do know is that you…unnerve me. One minute, I can't think unless you're standing near, and the next minute, I can't form a coherent thought until you move away. Two days ago, I had a really strong handle on my life, my job and my future. Now, I'm spinning downward in some dark, dangerous whirlpool. I've done that before, Nick, and the results nearly killed me. I'm not going there again. Not for anyone."

He took a tentative step forward. "We're connected to each other, Danielle. By forces neither one of us fully understand. You can't just send me away."

Her eyebrows popped up so high, they disappeared into her wispy bangs. "Want to bet?"

10

EVEN THOUGH NICK had already left the building, Danielle took great pleasure in slamming the door behind him. Who did he think she was, anyway? The vulnerable, spoiled rotten, rich-girl princess her parents had tried to raise her to be, unable to take care of herself, unwilling to put herself on the line for the few people who trusted her? She'd made a lot of mistakes in her life, but dammit, she'd lived on the streets for five years and survived. Sure, she'd had help from Micki. A lot of help from Micki. Okay, truth be told, if not for her best friend, she would have died and never had the chance to reconcile with her brother, get straight and start a new life.

The realization deflated her anger to mild annoyance. She stalked back to her desk, determined to keep things in perspective. Yes, she'd had help, but kicking her drug habit had been her demon to conquer, her personal victory. And despite that she had no experience whatsoever, her project had been ahead of schedule and on budget until this morning. She'd won the confidence of a crusty crew of construction workers, who treated her with respect. And she had a growing circle of friends, from Micki and Margo to the Divines, to Armand—

friends so unlike the ones she'd latched on to before, friends who wouldn't sell her out for a hit of speed.

She certainly didn't need Nick Davis reminding her of what a screwup she'd once been. Nick Davis wasn't even his real name, for Pete's sake. No, he was Nicholai Vaux, a mysterious gypsy who'd so far given her two fantastic sexual experiences without ever touching her—and who desperately loved a woman who no longer existed.

On the other hand, he was also the man who'd stood beside her today without uttering one word, lending quiet, unwavering support. A man whose talent fascinated her, and who seemed genuinely interested in her safety and success. A man she'd unceremoniously thrown out of her life simply because he cared.

Danielle wandered to the coffeepot and filled a foam cup with the dregs of the pot Nick had brewed before her interview with the police detective. She sat at her desk as her digital clock blinked away the time. The insurance adjusters had come and gone. The new security team would arrive in the next hour, and Doyle had insisted on prepping them himself. She'd spoken to her brother, who'd assured her that all construction projects experienced setbacks from time to time. The Divines had also expressed concern only about the safety of the workers and were much more focused on the ten-thousand-dollar-a-plate fund-raiser they were planning tonight for the governor of the state. For the moment, Danielle had nothing to do and nowhere to go, so naturally, her thoughts returned to Nick, the one man who perplexed her, frustrated her and fascinated her all at the same time.

There was so much about his claims she didn't understand. No matter how much she tried to find a logical explanation for her experience the night before, she
couldn't come up with a plausible rationalization.
She'd been in that woman's body. The echoes of her
increased heart rate still pounded in her head. Every
wisp of cold air across her skin, every trickle of icy
water, every warm breath, hot kiss and hard thrust had
been as real as the cup of lukewarm coffee she held in
her hands right now. Somehow, Nick had transported
her into another woman's body. The sensual power of
the experience still sizzled beneath her skin. Just the
thought of how he'd licked her nipples in the water
made her tight, hard and wet.

She'd wanted Nick from the moment she'd met him.
Now that she'd tasted him, even in a dreamlike state,
the craving had intensified. Maybe she hadn't really
been angry with him a few minutes ago because of his
dictatorial tone. Maybe she was just terrified of a lust
she couldn't shake.

Maybe she'd better do something about that lust—
something real. Tangible. Immediate.

A knock at the door startled her. She jumped, sending the coffee all over her desk. She shouted for the
visitor to come in as she scrambled for paper towels.

"You always were a klutz," Micki said, entering the
office in her favorite Kate Spade "Looker" boots, a
red miniskirt with matching crop top and a hard hat
perched saucily over her slick black bob.

Danielle told Micki where she could shove her sarcasm. If she wasn't her best friend in the entire world,

she might have knocked her out on her barely covered ass just to drive the point home.

"Does my brother know you dress like a slut?"

Micki leveled her with a bitchy grin, prepared to trade as many barbs with Danielle as necessary to re-establish their usual repartee. From the moment they'd met six years ago when Danielle was a fifteen-year-old runaway and Micki was on the verge of breaking free of the street life, they'd acted like sisters. Sniping and clawing at one another one minute, loving each other unconditionally the next. Danielle didn't much care if Bas and Micki hadn't yet made their live-in relationship legal. Micki was already family as far as she was concerned.

But the wedding was on the horizon, judging by the big honkin' rock Micki now wore on her left ring finger.

"Bas bought the outfit for me himself. Wanted me to make an impression on the wedding planners."

Danielle snorted. "The Divines are doing your wedding. They already know you're a hard-ass."

Micki swung around and pushed out her derriere so the snug wool material stretched over her impressively shaped backside. "Yeah, but it's a great, hard ass. Should be. Takes an hour of Pilates every day to keep it that way." She wiggled into a chair, then kicked her boots onto the top of Danielle's desk. "Was so much easier to keep my figure when I couldn't afford to eat."

Just a few moments in Micki's presence and Danielle relaxed. She tossed the stale coffee in the sink of her private bathroom, then drew a chair around her desk to sit beside her friend. God, how she needed to talk to someone she trusted, just shoot the shit and be nasty and bitchy and real. Micki could give as good as she got and spouting off with each other tended to make them nicer to the public at large.

"Why are you here? Did Bas send you?" Danielle asked.

Micki answered her with a look that said, essentially, *duh.*

"Is he worried I'll relapse because of all the new pressure?"

Micki rubbed a smudge of concrete dust off the black leather panel on her boot. Two-tone in black and red, the knee-high boots made her legs look sleek and slim.

"He'll be worried about you relapsing for the rest of your life, but that doesn't mean he has no faith in you. It just means he understands how hard your battle has been. And that he doesn't expect you to be perfect."

The iciness that had gathered around Danielle's heart since her tantrum with Nick cracked a bit. She often wondered how her life would have turned out if she'd had her brother's unconditional love on a daily basis while growing up, instead of receiving it only in the last year. But she kept the speculation short. The past couldn't be changed.

Could it?

She swung around to Micki. "Do you believe in reincarnation?"

Micki yanked her feet off the desk, nearly tumbling from her chair in her haste. "Excuse me? How did we get from my sexy boots and your sexy brother to the decidedly unsexy topic of reincarnation?''

Danielle snapped her fingers in quick, rapid succession. ''Gotta keep with the conversation, babe.''

Micki's sapphire eyes, so much more brilliant and blue than Danielle's own pale shade of cornflower, narrowed with speculation. ''Are we getting spiritual all of a sudden?''

Danielle shrugged. She wouldn't go that far. She'd never known a day of religion in her life. Her parents had worshipped at the church of the almighty dollar. Her brother, while wealthy, didn't seem so devoted to money, but if he had a spiritual value system, Danielle had no idea what it was. Bas was a painfully private man. That Danielle knew him at all seemed a miracle of sorts, and one she was deeply grateful for.

But Micki, who'd been raised with church and Sunday school and traditional sacraments, had lost her religion a long time ago. Her own journey had been so much like Danielle's. Tragedy and betrayal had shaken their belief in anything beyond survival. People like them tended to count on only what they could see with their own eyes or steal with their own hands. But what Nick had proposed to her last night was a concept she couldn't quite get her mind around. Could her friend help her make sense of a senseless situation?

''I'm just curious if you think your soul dies with you, then goes to some separate spiritual plane or returns to earth to work out issues from previous lives.''

Micki's eyes widened and she sat up straight, her feet on the floor and her hands in her lap. ''Such an easy question," she quipped. "After I answer it, do I get a prize? Like maybe, the Nobel?"

"I'm not kidding, Mick."

Micki ran her fingers through her hair. "I can see that. We haven't been off the streets that long, Danielle. I haven't really worked out the mysteries of life, yet. You had it rougher than I did, so I don't think you should expect to have it all figured out, either."

Danielle frowned. Her older, wiser friend was supposed to know this stuff, wasn't she? "You used to at least know what you believed in," she reminded her. "And what you didn't."

Micki chuckled. "Of course, I did. Life was a lot simpler when all I had to do was concentrate on surviving." Micki turned and grabbed Danielle's hands, nearly nicking her with the diamond on her engagement ring. Her brother really didn't understand the concept of understated.

"Maybe that's what you're going through right now," she continued. "You finally have some stability in your life, so you have time to think about things you never would have bothered with before. Not too long ago, the only thing you had time to worry about was your next meal or your next hit."

Danielle nodded automatically, not knowing how to explain to her best friend about Nick or his magic bottle. If she confessed, would Micki think she'd started using again?

"Okay, but at least tell me this—do you think that the concept of reincarnation is possible?"

Micki drummed her fingers on Danielle's knuckles. "There are whole religions with thousands of followers who believe in reincarnation. Who am I to say their beliefs are wrong and mine are right?''

''Then you don't believe in reincarnation?''

''Not personally,'' Micki confessed, ''though I can understand the need to believe that you get more than one chance at life, that you can learn and grow and fix your screwups as time progresses. However,'' she said with the kind of pause Danielle knew would be followed by a wisecrack, ''I really can't understand what anyone would learn if they came back as a bug.''

They laughed comfortably, chatted some more about life and destiny. Danielle decided not to say anything to Micki about Nick or his outrageous claims, but she did decide that she couldn't simply ignore or push aside this mystery. Even without the bottle in her possession any longer, the connection between her and Nick remained strong. She had to figure out the truth, if for no other reason than to get him out of her life—past, present and future.

THE PHONE CALL had come as a complete surprise. Nicholai thought for sure that the confrontation with Danielle in her office had set him back weeks in his quest to break down the boundaries between the past and the present. He still wasn't sure exactly what they'd argued about. Yes, he should have toned down his tyrannical tone, but she'd reacted with more anger than warranted. Even his Sofia, a hot-blooded female of legendary temper, would never have reacted with such venom, not unless sufficiently provoked. Danielle, on the other hand, faced more stress and responsibility than his beloved wife ever had. The gypsy life was inherently more simple.

So when Danielle had called him and asked him to stop by Divine Events and pick up a package that had been left there by one of the partners and bring it to her at the construction site, he'd obliged.

When he arrived at the restaurant site, a security guard asked for his name, then after double-checking a list he carried on a clipboard, waved him through. The main dining area looked no less a war zone than it had this afternoon, except that work lights had been placed throughout the space so that no dark corners or shadows existed. Nowhere for vandals to hide. He looked for Danielle in her office, but when he found the door locked, he knew of only one other place to find her.

Unlike the rest of the restaurant interior, the VIP room had light from only one lamp—a strong, directed bulb that illuminated a generous portion of one wall. The spherical pink splash of color he'd seen this morning now had shape. Two unmistakably nude bodies, entwined in a breathless kiss.

Danielle stood a few feet away, lingering in the shadow behind the light stand, admiring the work.

Her work, he amended, noticing her smock and the brushes in her hands. An artist? The knowledge stopped him cold.

"Sofia used to paint," he said, louder than he'd planned.

Danielle turned and rewarded his honesty with a smile. "Did she? What did she paint? Murals?"

He shook his head, stunned. Over the past twenty-four hours, he'd noted difference upon difference between his lost love and Danielle Stone. In the back of his mind, he now realized that he'd started to doubt the theory he'd come to Chicago to prove.

But now, he'd learned of Danielle's talent, so like his wife's, and he was thrown into another round of uncertainty.

"She painted portraits, actually."

Danielle nodded. "Did she sell her work?"

"No, never. She liked to linger over her subjects, sketch them from all angles, exploring a full range of facial expressions before she committed one drop of paint to a canvas. She gave the portraits as gifts and rarely even signed her name."

A shy smile bloomed on Danielle's face. "It was her secret passion, then."

He stepped toward her. "Her only one. She was an open book, my Sofia. She couldn't lie." The claim made him chuckle. Despite her innate honesty, Sofia had managed to lie successfully for the duration of their affair, prior to her plea to her father that had resulted in the breaking of her betrothal to Milosh. "Well, mostly, she couldn't lie."

"Definitely can't say the same about me. I've been a first-rate liar for too long."

"That's not true anymore."

"You don't know that."

"Yes, I do. You were honest with me last night about parts of your past I'm sure you'd like to forget."

"I was trying to scare you off."

"It didn't work."

Danielle closed her eyes and her shoulders sagged

with the weight of his words. When she opened her eyes again, her sweet blue irises gleamed with emotion. He had to root his feet to the floor to keep from pulling her into his arms.

He watched her throat bob with a painful swallow, as if telling him the truth scraped against her throat. "No matter what I saw last night, no matter what I felt, no matter that believing what you propose would explain so much about my past, I can't accept that I'm somehow the reincarnated soul of a woman you once loved. It's impossible."

"No, Danielle. It's not. We are proof."

"We? How did you ever accept that you are the reincarnated soul of her husband?"

Nick stopped and placed the bag he'd retrieved from Divine Events at her feet. With raised eyebrows, he weighed the possibility of telling her the truth. If she was having so much trouble accepting the likelihood that she possessed a reincarnated soul, how could she understand that his soul was one and the same? He was Nicholai Vaux. He himself had loved Sophia one hundred years ago.

"I've never had to accept the truth, Danielle. I've simply always known."

He hated the sound of the half truth, but he could think of no other way to broach the topic without ending their relationship, such that it was, forever. Admitting to her that he'd been murdered and then had, through magic, managed to come back to life, would likely send her running as far away from him as she could. What would be the point? How he'd returned to her was not important. He had to remain focused on developing the connection they'd reestablished in the past two days.

She'd summoned him here tonight. Without the influence of the bottle, she'd sought him out. The anger she directed at him earlier seemed to have dissipated, replaced by a mood that bordered on melancholy, yet hovered close to quiet curiosity, just like when she'd come to see him last night. She was a brave woman. The questions and confusion he'd witnessed last night seemed to have calmed, as if she'd accepted at least part of the truth, as if she only needed a bit more help to guide her the rest of the way.

"Sounds so easy," she answered.

He blew out a breath and shook his head. "Easy is not the word I'd choose. There's nothing simple about turning your life upside down because of a belief you can't prove, one that goes against every belief you've ever had your entire life." He stepped around the bag. The heat from the lamp sizzled and a trickle of sweat formed around his collar. "After I saw your photograph in that magazine, everything in my life changed. I knew who you were, and yet, you were a stranger. I'd just started to settle down in Georgia, make a life for myself. Then suddenly, I'm on the road to a state I've never been to, a city I'd practically never heard of, all to chase down a woman who would likely have me committed to a mental institution once I told her my story."

He moved away from the heat of the lamp and stood directly behind her. The scent of the paint on her hands and on the brushes she held lax between her fingers, assailed his nostrils, enhancing her natural spicy perfume with the distinctive aroma of artistry. How many times had he caught a similar whiff on Sofia's skin? How many times had the essence driven him insane with lust?

Too many times to count, this evening included.

He moved to back away, but she reached behind and grabbed his hand, smearing his skin with a soft ochre pigment that had lingered on her fingers. The paint was slick and oily, and against his warm flesh, innately sensual. He couldn't stop from rubbing the spot where they touched, blending the splattered drop of paint across the outside of her hand.

"Don't leave, Nick."

He leaned forward. She leaned her full weight against him, so that the gentle curve of her back pressed against his chest, and the soft swell of her hips and buttocks teased his erection.

"I couldn't leave, even if you asked me. Even if you begged."

She spun around slowly, careful to maintain contact so that her breasts brushed against his chest and her thighs pressed against his jeans. "Does that mean you can't take no for an answer?"

Her tone was light, teasing. So like Sofia's, and yet, entirely different.

He grinned. "I wouldn't know."

She smoothed her tongue over her teeth, then reversed the direction on her lips. The wetness she spread increased the glossiness on her mouth and made him hunger to taste once again what he'd craved for a century.

"Hasn't any woman ever told you no?" she asked.

"Not that I recall."

He heard a wooden clatter as the brushes she'd been holding dropped from her hands. In the next instant, she'd grabbed his backside and yanked him close, with a hard demand that shot his blood temperature to a dangerous level.

"Well, you won't be hearing it tonight, either. We're going to lay things on the line, Nicholai Vaux," she said, pronouncing every syllable of his name perfectly, as if she'd spoken the Romany name every night for the past hundred years. "Nothing brings us together tonight but us. No magic. No tricks. Just passion." She lifted onto her tiptoes and swiped a kiss across his chin. "Just need. Is that enough for you?"

With a growl, Nicholai grabbed her waist and pulled her up, pausing only to answer her question before he devoured her, starting with her mouth.

"With you, nothing will be enough."

11

As NICK SWUNG her toward the bed, still captured in his arms, Danielle's feet connected with the package she'd sent him to fetch from Divine Events. She'd had everything so perfectly planned—the privacy, the lighting, the mood—the ultimate seduction. She'd planned to lure him here, drive him wild with passion and make love to him as if the world would end tomorrow. She'd force them to a crossroads. Did he want her or the woman he believed she'd been in a previous life? She knew of only one way to find out.

She'd had enough of making love on the phone or in a dream. She wanted the real deal, right now.

And he seemed eager to oblige.

Unexpectedly, his never-ending kiss knocked her plan right out of her head. As he set her down, his tongue teased hers, dueling and retreating, building a hunger she couldn't sate. His hands roamed softly and stealthily, igniting fires that smoldered rather than flamed. The moment she registered his palm brushing over her breast, it was gone, smoothing a path down her belly. Just when she thought he'd dip his fingers between her legs, the pressure appeared beneath her bottom, cupping her with sweet possessiveness. By the time she finally pushed him away, she was hot and panting for breath.

His sinful smile swiped even that little bit of air away.

"Tell me you don't want me," he commanded.

"That would be a lie," she answered, pressing her fingers on her lips in an attempt to quell the vibrations stemming from his kiss. She sat up straighter, determined to harness this seduction back under her control. "Why do you think I called you here?"

He glanced over his shoulder at the abandoned paper bag. "You needed the package from Divine Events."

"But why did I call you? You'd know if you peeked."

His expression neither acknowledged nor denied. "I did wonder what was so important that you'd keep me from my carving."

She smiled, her confidence increasing. "There are some things only a man like you can provide."

From the moment she'd made the decision this afternoon to seduce Nick Davis, she'd known she first had to create an air of mystery of her own. With all the magical secrets surrounding him, Nick affected her in ways she didn't understand. With him, she did things she'd never dream of doing, believed things she'd never imagine believing. She had to take the upper hand. If she simply surrendered completely to him, she'd never know if the passion surging through her was real, or just another one of his unexplainable tricks or raw seductive influence.

The thought sent her mind spiraling. What if the bag didn't contain her special order from Gia Divine? What if Nick had pulled a switch, replacing the specialty food item she'd ordered with the powerful perfume bottle? She couldn't allow that. There could be no magic tonight except what they wove with their own bodies.

"Bring me the bag," she said, pointing.

He obliged, scooping up the parcel and tossing it lightly to her on the bed. She tore into the crumbled paper, grinning when she found the six small jars she'd requested from the Divines' head chef. Over the last year, the Divines had developed quite a reputation for appealing to the sensual desires of their clients. They'd filled a niche market by hosting romantic parties lavish with exotic foods and drinks, the very menu that would be the cornerstone of Pillow Talk once it opened. During Danielle's brief stint as a receptionist for Divine Events, she'd been shocked at how many people came into the shop simply to order a dozen chocolate Grand Marnier-coated strawberries or arrange for the delivery of a decadent dish called Spiced Pearls, famous for the fire the saucy steamed oysters ignited in the mouth, and in other areas of the body. Despite that Danielle had experimented in many ways with her art since her return to Chicago, she'd never imagined that she'd call Gia Divine with an order for a rush delivery of her edible body paints, appropriately named "Palette for Sin."

But then again, she'd never imagined she'd meet a man like Nick, either.

She had to do this her way. She'd dug into one of her most forbidden secret fantasies, hoping this test would prove whether the passion and trust she felt toward Nick was real. She remembered how Armand had once bought her a set of paints somewhat like these from a Parisian sex shop. He'd regaled her with illicit promises of extreme pleasure—two artists using each other's bodies as canvases, then licking their masterpieces to full climax. But she'd never taken him up on the offer, making excuse after excuse until the game had finally been forgotten.

As sexually adventurous as she and Armand had been, combining her love for paint and her sexual desires stepped over a line Danielle hadn't been prepared to cross—until tonight. The idea had popped into her head unbidden, as if her subconscious had hoarded the idea until she met exactly the right man.

Her soul mate, perhaps?

She shook the thought away as she upended the bag and the six twist-top jars spilled onto the bed, along with fresh, clean brushes of soft sable with rounded heads and feathery tips, perfect for what she had in mind. As she unbuttoned the smock she'd thrown over her clothes earlier, she glanced up at Nick through her lashes. He stood beside the bed, hands on his hips, confusion in his eyes.

Good. It was his turn to be caught off-guard.

"What have you got there?"

He reached for the nearest jar, the magenta shade Gia had named "Raspberry Rush," but Danielle snagged the paint away before he could grab hold.

"A surprise. A chance to try something different."

She tore away the smock, then ripped off her T-shirt. His eyes widened at the sight of her lacy blue bra. In an instant, his irises darkened beyond their original black, unfathomable with pure desire.

Her nipples hardened, pushed upward against the demi-cup. Her heart raced, chasing her pure physical reaction with a rush of blood that pumped into every pulse in her body. She licked her lips and eased toward him, looking forward to this seduction just as much as she looked forward to driving Nick to madness.

"Your turn," she said.

"Excuse me?"

"The shirt. Take it off."

With one arched eyebrow, he complied with her request. He removed the buttons from the slits in the material with painful slowness, focusing his gaze on her as he worked. He ripped the material off his shoulders in one quick movement, revealing a chest hard with muscle and lightly dusted with dark hair. His male nipples were flat and round and her tongue ached to swirl around the shape until he went wild with wanting.

With a tentative touch, she ran her finger along the edge of his waistband. "Now the jeans. I need a full canvas to work with."

"You're going to paint me?"

With a determined pluck, she undid the snap on his jeans. "Not like anyone else ever has, I'll bet."

She stretched around him so that her shoulder skimmed across his bare back as she reached for the towel she'd hung over a stool. She wiped away the last of the real paint she'd had on her hands, wanting to start with a fresh palette. She pressed a button on her portable stereo, engaging the cool strains of the jazz guitar CD she favored while painting. Nothing exotic or instrumentally challenging, just soft, rhythmic strumming that soothed her muse and lured her to the surface.

When Danielle turned, Nick had done exactly as she'd asked. He'd removed every stitch of clothing and the sight of him naked, hard and willing nearly stole her breath. She reached out and turned the lamp, not toward him, but away, so that his exquisite body glimmered in the shadows.

"I'm not shy, Danielle," he said, stepping forward. "I'll stand in the light if you wish."

She grabbed a tinted swatch of thin cheesecloth and threw it over the bright light. "Lighting is essential to an artist. Stay where you are. You'll know when I've got it just right."

She moved two more tall lamps closer, draped the bulbs, then switched on the lights until the room was bathed in a muted, golden glow. She pulled out a clean palette and lifted a fresh folded tarp, then dropped it at his feet.

Hands on his hips, he watched her work with quiet amusement, completely comfortable despite his lack of clothes. She circled him as she poured the paints onto the palette. First Raspberry Rush, then Guilty Grape, followed by Pineapple Prickle, Citrus Sensation and Spicy Chili-Mint. The strong scents of the flavored paints teased her nostrils and coaxed a persistent hunger from deep in her belly.

She grabbed a brush, but couldn't quite decide what to paint, or where to begin. She circled Nick, who remained curious but still as she perused him head to toe. She couldn't push away the perfect symmetry between what he looked like now and how he'd appeared in the vision she'd had last night. If he hadn't insisted that the scene she'd witnessed had happened over a century ago, she would have bet her last chocolate truffle that he was the same man, right down to the thumbprint-sized birthmark low on his groin.

After her second rotation, he crossed his arms and turned to watch her as she retrieved the last jar of paint from the bed.

"Aren't you ready to start?" he asked, clearly impatient.

She didn't face him when she spoke, but the edge in his voice sent a warm vibration up her spine. "Got someplace to go?"

He chuckled. "Not exactly, but I'm not the most patient man."

"You claim you've waited one hundred years to find me. What's a few more minutes?"

He harrumphed, and she bit down a giggle.

"What about the guards outside?" he countered. "I don't suppose you instructed them not to walk in without announcing themselves."

She grinned. "I'm an artist, not an exhibitionist, Nick. I gave them very direct orders not to come in here unless the building was on fire. Besides, the door locked behind you when you shut it."

"And so I'm just supposed to wait here while you prepare your little tubs of paint?"

She twisted the top off the final color, "Black Velvet," inhaling the rich chocolate aroma that assailed her nostrils with instant power. She tossed the top onto the floor, intending to use this hue until the very last drop.

She retrieved a brush from her pocket, then dipped it in the jar, dousing it generously. "I'm done preparing, Nick. Now it's your turn to get ready."

"For what?"

She swiped the tip of the paintbrush across her tongue and groaned with appreciation of the dark, chocolate flavor. As she stirred the brush back into the jar to replenish her medium, Nick's eyes narrowed, then widened in realization.

"What is that paint?"

She leveled him with a disbelieving stare. "Haven't you ever heard of edible body paint?"

His arms tightened over his chest. "No."

She sashayed so close to him, her breath teased the hair on his chest "Oh, man. You're in for one heck of a sensual surprise, then. When I said I was going to paint *you*, I meant that literally. I'm going to let my artistic sensibilities take me where no other woman has likely gone before. You're going to be my masterpiece."

He cleared his throat. "And then? Art is to be admired, not touched."

She flicked the tip of the brush across the edge of his shoulder. "Says who?"

NICHOLAI HISSED with pleasure as the paintbrush glided over his skin. The cold paint injected the air with the sweet scent of chocolate, teasing his senses to life. He swallowed deeply and couldn't break his gaze from

Danielle, whose blue eyes glittered with naughty delight.

"Such an expansive canvas I have here," she said, drawing her brush across his chest, stopping at the half-way point above his heart to replenish the paint. "I don't quite know what to do with you."

He snagged her gaze with a look of complete disbelief. He might be a man jettisoned out of time and place by magic, but he wasn't naive. She knew exactly what she was doing. She'd devised a form of torture he didn't yet know how to react to. Yes, he knew that in this new century, sexual toys and games were commonplace. He'd seen catalogues that featured underwear that could be nibbled off and massage oils in countless flavors, some that even brought heat to the skin when rubbed. He guessed that at some point, he'd seen an advertisement for paints that could be applied to the body for sensual pleasure, but never in one million years, much less one hundred, would he have dreamed he'd provide the canvas for a lover's brush.

To Nicholai, sex was an intimacy meant to be shared between lovers, not a sport or temporary diversion. He knew the world at large had changed their views on that topic in the last few decades, but until this moment, Nicholai hadn't realized how his views had *not* changed.

And yet, the thought of denying her this pleasure—of denying himself—seemed incomprehensible.

"Start where you like," he told her. "I suppose you need me to remain still?"

She twirled the brush in the paint, then applied a

series of lines across his stomach. The action tickled, but he willed himself not to react.

"As still as you can," she answered. "I wouldn't want to ruin my creation before I'm ready to lick it off."

Trading the jar and brush for the palette she'd prepared, she splashed a few more lines of color on his torso. When she made a mistake, or at least, pretended to, she licked the offending color away. She spent a ridiculous amount of time deciding precisely what hue looked best on his nipples. Nicholai had never known he was so sensitive there until she'd teased and tasted him until near insanity.

By the time she dropped her attention to his sex, he was hard and rigid with wanting. He watched her hover the paintbrush around the head of his penis, "Raspberry Rush" thick on the bristles.

The moment she made contact, his entire body became enflamed and he wouldn't have been surprised if the cool gel started to sizzle with the heat emanating from his skin. She dropped to her knees and coated him completely, all the while commenting on the perfect shape and size of her canvas.

"Hmm…I've never tried the *impasto* technique on something so impressive."

He swallowed, trying to form a coherent phrase while she tortured him with sweet, measured strokes. "What does that mean?"

She dipped the brush back into the palette. "It's a method of applying paint very, very thickly. And these paints do it so well. But the scent is driving me insane. Do you like raspberries, Nick?" She looked up at him with narrowed eyes. "I love raspberries. Especially when dipped with chocolate."

She dropped the brush and reached up, scooping a layer of the chocolate-flavored paint from his navel and smearing it on the tip of his sex. She licked her lips in anticipation and Nick feared he might lose his footing when she moved forward and took a taste from the head of his erection.

"Oh, my," she groaned. "Delicious."

He thought she'd end the torment there, but she did not. Instead, she took great, guttural pleasure in licking every drop of paint off his cock, smearing her cheeks and chin with the thick, red flavoring. When she took him fully into her mouth, he had to grab the nearby bedpost in order to remain standing. Pleasure struck with lightning force and he couldn't help but weave his hands into her hair and surrender to her sweet assault.

The moment she broke away from him, he cupped her cheeks and lifted her so he could taste her for himself. The remnants of the raspberry and chocolate paints were musky and sweet on her lips, and the combination of flavors on her hot moist tongue kicked his desire into overdrive. When he pulled her fully against him in the kiss, the paint smeared from his body to hers and without patience, he removed her bra, jeans and panties until she was as bared to him as he'd been to her.

"You're a wicked woman," he said, grinding his mouth against her neck as he spoke.

She laughed as she clutched at his buttocks and shifted so that his sex pressed hard against hers. Her slickness summoned him so that he nearly slipped inside her without a moment's hesitation.

But he pulled back. He'd allowed her to control the seduction to this point, but he had to draw a line. He wanted to be inside her, but first, he wanted to drive her as wild with wanting as she had him.

With a measured twist, he tumbled her onto the bed and then snagged the palette from where she'd left it on the floor. She crawled backward, away from him, her eyes wide and laughter spilling from her lips.

"Now, wait a minute. I'm the artist, here."

Nick threw the brush aside and dipped his fingers into the gooey colors. "I'm a quick study. Besides, I'm not going to attempt any kind of masterwork. I just want to make you come."

He smeared his fingers down her body, creating a rainbow trail from between her breasts to the base of her thighs. He eased beside her on the bed and made quite the production out of swirling the citrus-scented orange over her areola, dabbing a drop of the minty green on each nipple. She sat up quickly and would have bolted if he hadn't grabbed her by the arms.

"Can't take what you dish out, hmm?"

"No!" she insisted. "The green has chili flavoring in it. It's hot!"

He grinned, certain the body paint was entirely safe, even if the sensation was a tad disconcerting.

"You started this, Danielle. You can't deny me a taste of you just because the flavor I choose isn't to your liking. Or is it?"

Her breast tasted like heaven. The tangy citrus melded with the spicy chili-mint, sending his tastebuds into pure delight. The feel of her rigid nipple between his teeth only intensified the sensation, especially once she started moaning in delight. He grew hungrier and hungrier as her breathing grew more shallow. As her moans amplified, her writhing on the bed created a frenzy of movement he longed to match. He followed the rainbow downward and once he dipped his mouth into her sweet center, he knew he'd found the most delicious flavor of all.

He laved her lips, parted her with his fingers, then dipped deep inside with his tongue. She bucked beneath him, but she didn't pull away, not until the brink was just one flick away.

"The bag!" she cried, moving back on the bed, out of his reach.

"What?"

She pointed desperately to where the package that had contained the paints lay on the floor. "Get it, Nick. Please!"

He complied, certain there was nothing else they needed, but he couldn't tell her no. Panting, Danielle dug inside and found what she'd so desperately wanted—a small square packet Nick instantly recognized.

"A condom?" he asked, surprised. "I didn't know the Divines provided such complete service."

She tore the packet open. "Great sex is safe sex, you know."

He plucked the condom from her fingers and kissed away her protest. "I haven't been with a woman in…" A century? Couldn't say that now, could he? "…a very long time. We don't need this modern contraption."

Nick wanted desperately to feel Danielle flesh to flesh, unhampered by even the thinnest of layers between them.

She grabbed the packet away from him and broke the kiss, softening her stubbornness with a wink. ''No sleeve, you leave. This isn't just about you or about diseases. It's about me, my past and my desire to not be a parent anytime soon. Come on, Nick. You don't want to end this here and now, do you?''

What was she, insane?

He climbed onto the bed. She removed the circle from the packet, then rolled it expertly over his sex, taking the time to stroke him.

Now wasn't the time to argue or ask for explanations. At this moment, and likely every moment afterward, he'd give her whatever she wanted, whenever she asked. The sensation was not entirely unpleasurable. The latex fit snugly against his skin and a slick lubricant incited a unique friction between her hands and his flesh.

With one heavy gasp, Danielle straddled him and they fell back into a kiss. Nick renewed his adoration of her body by caressing her breasts, her arms, her back, her belly. He caught his breath when she shifted so that his sex could ease into her soft heat.

Time stilled. For an instant, Nick thought someone had punched him in the gut, the sensation was so overpowering, so familiar—and yet, so infinitesimally unique. Their bodies eased together, melded, then merged, with every nerve ending electrified, every sense enhanced. The scent of the air shifted and weighed heavier in his lungs as he inhaled.

"Nicholai?"

A flash of fear passed over Danielle's features, but before Nick could say a word, she shifted and the atmosphere changed with her. She grabbed his hands, threw her head back and moved atop him with complete and utter abandon. She milked his body with her undulations, and when her own pleasure nearly overtook her, he braced her hips so they could both hold on until the end. The final thrust resulted in an explosion, two pure and wild orgasms crying into the night.

He had no idea how much time had passed until she started to shiver. The room was hot thanks to the lighting, but she quivered as if she'd been out in the bitter cold of winter. Nick rolled her over and tugged on the edges of the comforter until they were swathed in silk.

He must have dozed off, because when he opened his eyes again, she was gone.

"Danielle?"

She came out of a door in the corner, her clothes sticking to her as if her skin was damp, rubbing a towel over wet hair. "Hey."

"You showered?"

She smiled. "Pillow Talk has all the amenities, including a private bathroom with a shower. You're free to use it, too."

"I'd rather have used it with you."

Still grinning, she climbed onto the bed beside him and used her damp towel to wipe away the last remnants of the body paint. "I thought about that, but you were sleeping so soundly, I didn't want to wake you up. I might, however," she dabbed a kiss on his cheek, "be convinced to shower again, if the incentive is right."

With a growl, he pulled her into his arms and kissed her. The private bathroom must have had mouthwash too, because the cool mint taste awakened his taste-buds, whetting his appetite for another sample of chili-mint green.

He was reaching for the discarded palette when someone pounded on the door and a frantic male voice shouted Danielle's name.

"Damn it!" she said, tearing off the bed and stomping toward the door. She swung it open without regard to the fact that Nick was lying on the bed, naked, be-hind her. "I thought I told you guys not to interrupt me unless the building was on fire!"

The security guard looked slightly chagrined. "Yes, ma'am. That's the problem. We've got a fire and we need to get you out of here."

12

DANIELLE BLINKED TWICE, certain her new security guard was kidding. But the way his brown eyes kept glancing anxiously toward the front exit told her he wasn't.

"Where are the other guards?" she asked.

"Checking things out. Richard smelled smoke during a routine walk-through in the kitchen."

Danielle tossed her towel behind her and forked her fingers through her wet hair, vaguely aware that Nick was jumping into his clothes at lightning speed. "The appliances aren't hooked up yet."

"Could be wiring," the guard guessed. "Could be coming from outside. Either way, we need to get the hell out of here until the fire department comes. I just called."

One quick glance told her Nick was dressed, so she spun back into the room to grab her boots and hard hat. She pointed to the guard as she worked through the laces. "I don't smell smoke and I don't hear my alarms. This could be a setup, designed to get us out of the building so serious damage can be done. Stand by the front door, so you can evacuate if you need to. But don't leave the building until flames are licking at your shoes, do you hear me?"

He nodded, but Danielle wasn't sure if he'd follow her directive, which she'd partly exaggerated. She didn't want to put any of her people in danger, but one of the first systems they'd put in place once they'd pulled permits was the fire alarm. The engineers and the insurance adjuster had both double-checked the system this afternoon. Since it had been in perfect working order, they'd declared that the blowtorches simply hadn't created enough flame or smoke to set off the alarms—which made sense since there'd been no smoke or fire damage. Whatever fire or smoke the guards smelled tonight likely wasn't coming from inside.

"I don't suppose I could convince you to stay with the guard by the front door while I check this out," Nick said, his arms crossed over his shirt. A smear of "Raspberry Rush" on his chest peeked out at the vee of his collar.

With a rebellious lick, Danielle removed the telltale sign of their lovemaking session. God, the sex had been amazing. Mind-blowing. Time-bending. She had so much to process, even her brief shower hadn't given her enough of a break to piece together all she'd seen and felt. And there wasn't time now. Her future actions and reactions depended entirely on her ability to separate fact from fiction, truth from wishful thinking.

"You're learning about me, aren't you, Nick?" she asked, tying the last lace on her boot. "I'm not the type of woman to sit at a safe distance and do nothing."

He brushed her bangs out of her eyes. "No, you most certainly are not. You never have been."

Together, they made their way around the rubble of the fallen scaffolding and cut through the kitchen. They found one security guard holding the back door open while another pumped foam from an industrial-sized fire extinguisher into a burning Dumpster.

"Just a trash fire?" she asked.

"Looks that way," the security guard named Richard answered. "But Jimmy here thinks he saw someone."

Jimmy struggled with the fire extinguisher. The flames didn't seem to want to surrender to the chemical compound. Nick ran out beside him and disappeared behind one of the construction trailers, then returned with a second extinguisher. Together, they kept the fire from leaping to the old building or to any of the nearby flammable materials.

The fire department arrived soon after and put out the last of the flames with one concentrated blast from their hose. A crowd had gathered then quickly dispersed once they realized the show was over.

"Jimmy," Danielle addressed the guard as he sipped gingerly from a cold bottled water. "Richard said you saw someone? Who?"

Nick used a towel to wipe dirt and soot from his body. Between a hard day's work, the body paint and wrangling with the fire, the man needed a serious shower. And yet, Danielle couldn't imagine him looking any more delicious. He'd jumped right in to help without a moment's hesitation and other than one brief slipup this afternoon, he'd learned quickly that she wasn't the type who needed blind protecting, even when the danger was as real as a fire. A man who could learn fast and who possessed such sexual prowess and artistic talent had to be one in a million.

So why wasn't she feeling so lucky at this moment?

Jimmy cleared his throat. "I saw a woman."

"A woman? Where?"

With a limp armed gesture, Jimmy pointed to the end of the alley. "Down there. She ran away."

Danielle peered down the dark space between her building and the one behind it. The extra lighting she'd added to discourage thieves from hitting their supplies made a clear view into the alley difficult, if not impossible, because of the glare. "How could you see it was a woman?"

Jimmy smirked. "She ran like a girl. I've got sisters. I know this stuff."

Danielle snorted. The runner could have been an effeminate male, but now wasn't the time to point that out. She'd wait until the police completed their questioning.

Unfortunately, fifteen minutes later, the police finished the interviews without any solid leads. No one had seen or heard anything suspicious and the fire had done no real damage except to the plastic flip-top lid on the Dumpster. As far as the cops were concerned, vandals had struck again.

Danielle wasn't so sure.

She and Nick returned to the VIP room. Danielle glanced at the bed, remembering so vividly the power of their lovemaking. Not just because the orgasm had been unbelievable, but because of what she'd experienced the first moment their bodies had connected.

A memory.

Maybe. A flash of a picture, one she was sure she'd never seen before.

Had the vision popped out from the part of Sofia truly hidden inside her? Or had she been so caught up in the magic of their passion that she'd succumbed to wishful thinking?

She grabbed the sides of her head. This was too much! Too much to contemplate, too much to deal with. God, what she wouldn't have given for something to take the edge off, something to narrow her focus so she could concentrate on one of the many mysteries bouncing through her brain.

Only drugs wouldn't help. Her rational brain knew that. The drugs provided nothing but the illusion of clarity. She had to work through her problems with the skills she'd learned in rehab. And perhaps, with a little help from her friend.

Nick had stripped off his shirt and was poking his head into the private bathroom to check out the setup.

"Go on in," she encouraged him. "It's fairly luxurious, though all the fixtures aren't in and the decorating isn't done."

He stepped inside. She followed.

Steam from her shower still lingered in the air, as the exhaust fan wasn't yet working. The stall gleamed with white Italian marble tile and brushed silver fixtures, which included four showerheads, enclosed by a wall of thick, tempered glass. Two sinks, both with floating bowls on exquisitely designed pedestals, sat empty beneath flat fountains that would, once completed, continually burble water down the mosaic-tiled wall. The commode was hidden behind the dressing area, dominated by a full-sized, built-in vanity made of black granite.

Danielle remembered feeling very uneasy when she'd first seen the plans for the VIP room and the accompanying bathroom. Built for sin, she'd thought, but the Divines had assured her that such an amenity was all the rage in the hottest nightclubs. They'd decided to bring the vision of ultimate privacy into the restaurant. They wouldn't rent the room to just anyone. Only the highest profile celebrities and wealthiest power brokers would spend time in this fabulous suite.

But for now, it was a wonderland for her and Nick to enjoy.

Nick turned to face her. "I'm not sure I want to shower in here. I might stain the tile."

She laughed and smacked him playfully on the shoulder. "Don't worry. The cleaning crews will give this a final run-through before the place opens. I've showered here plenty of times when I was working late and had to be somewhere. Go ahead. Indulge yourself."

He pulled her flush against his body. The scent of smoke and chemicals assailed her, making her long for the musky, spicy scent she knew was beneath all the dirt and grime from the fire. Her mouth watered with the prospect of washing him clean herself.

"Join me," he invited.

"I've got to," she paused, allowing his lips to brush over hers in the promise of a kiss, "make a phone call."

His hands roamed down her back, massaging her

from shoulder to buttocks with his strong, deft fingers.
"It can wait."

"I want to talk to the Divines about the woman the
guards think they saw. Maybe they have some insight
into who she might have been."

Nick cocked an eyebrow. "Maybe it was one of the
Divines themselves."

The suggestion stopped the rush of pleasure coursing
through Danielle's veins from Nick's touch. "Why
would they try to torch their own restaurant?"

Nick shrugged. "I have no clue. It's just a thought."

Danielle leaned back against the nearest wall. Actually, there were plenty of reasons she could think of
once she put on her suspicious cap. Insurance fraud
blinked like a neon sign at the top of the list. The
Divines were incredibly tight for money since the purchase of the building and all three of them had shown
a marked disinterest in the construction to date. Still,
Danielle had been around during the initial planning
stages and work with the designers and the architects.
Their excitement then had been palpable. This restaurant was their dream.

"It can't be about money. They were doing fine until
they bought the building."

"Maybe the financial strain has been too much for
them."

Despite the logic, Danielle found herself shaking her
head. "No, they've weathered rougher times than this.
They started their party-planning business on their
own. No investors. In less than two years, they were
operating in the black. Things are tight now because
they put all their capital into the restaurant, but I know

they've taken on extra work at Divine Events to increase cash flow. And they have my brother backing them now. They aren't that cash strapped.''

Nick continued to unbutton his shirt, poking his head into the shower to test how to work the faucets and temperature controls.

''It wouldn't hurt to check their whereabouts tonight.''

''That'll be easy. All three of them are at that fundraiser at the Drake.'' She glanced at her watch. It was only ten o'clock. No way could any of them have ducked out before the dessert was served. Not without being noticed. ''Micki coordinates the bartenders for them. I'm pretty sure she was going, too. I'll call her.''

After he got two of the showerheads to blast hot water, he unbuckled his jeans. ''You do that.''

He enticed her with a grin that inspired her to hurry.

''You know where I'll be.''

NICK ALLOWED the scalding jets of water to pierce his skin until the sensations lulled his muscles into relaxation. The minute the guard had pounded on the door warning of fire, Nick's heart had been working on overdrive. Dying once in a fire was bad enough. Twice? He couldn't contemplate the irony.

Worst of all was knowing that Danielle could have been hurt as well. Sure, they'd caught the blaze before any serious damage had been done, but Nick wasn't stupid. The trailers out back contained propane tanks and much of the building was highly flammable. One gust of wind and the fire could have spread with deadly, rapid speed. At least he hadn't turned tail and run. He'd fought the flames with the fire extinguisher and had kept Danielle safe. Not like the last fire.

Not like then.

He'd been helpless, rendered unconscious by a rock to the skull. He hadn't come to until he, Jeta and Alexis had been bolted inside their *vardo* and the enclosed wagon lit on fire by the mob. They'd accused Alexis of witchcraft and condemned her to vigilante justice— all because she'd delivered a portentous warning about the drowning of a child.

Because of her vision, the child had lived, but Alexis had had to die. And her family with her.

For a split second, Nick felt the flames again. The excruciating pain, the sizzling hiss of burning skin, the choking blanket of smoke, the sickening odor of blood reaching the boiling point. He remembered thinking of Sofia just before he'd passed out—of knowing, hoping, praying, that they'd finally meet again in the Other-world.

He nearly cracked his head on the glass when Danielle sneaked in the shower behind him and placed her hand on his shoulder.

"Are you all right?"

He realized then he was shaking and mixed with the water was the sweat streaming from his pores. He managed to speak, which amazed even him.

"What did you find out?"

She looked at him skeptically, but answered his question while using a foamy sponge to soap his shoulders, chest, neck and back. "Micki stayed at the fund-raiser. She's there right now. None of the Divines left the room for more than a minute at a time. And I called

Bas. He has the resources to find out which specific competitors might be most interested in stopping our construction.''

Nick concentrated so that each word made sense, despite the throbbing in his brain. She spoke quickly, rushing through her explanation so she could get back to the topic that apparently interested her more—him.

For the first time since he'd known her, she was completely focused on him. She lovingly washed him from head to toe, dropping to her knees so she could stroke the sponge up and down his legs, missing nothing. Even when they'd made love, he'd sensed she'd possessed an agenda, a need beyond physical intimacy with him. She'd had a lot to prove, more than likely to herself, and he hadn't minded her second focus, knowing how difficult he'd made the task of concentration. Just one day ago, he'd told her she was the reincarnated soul of a woman who died in the last century and that magic and fate had combined to reunite them. He'd burdened her with so much, he was shocked she could focus on anything at all.

But once she'd washed and rinsed him clean, she stood. The concern in her eyes was as crystal clear as the blue of her irises. He swallowed, determined to shake the nightmares of his past and give the present his undivided attention.

He snared her around the waist with shaky hands and tugged her close. The contact with her sweet, clean flesh made him hard, needful. He took her mouth in a powerful kiss, and with one duel of tongues, the horrifying memories of his death by fire drizzled off his body and swirled down the drain.

She matched his need, his tempo. They kissed each other, aroused each other, until Nick knew nothing beyond the need to be inside her. He twisted, pressing her against the wall. She stopped him with shaky hands to his chest.

A moment sped by before he realized why she hesitated. He growled, grinding his cock against her belly. "I want you, Danielle."

The shower pelted them, the mist catching in her eyes and mouth. "I know, Nick. But we can't be stupid."

His need for her wouldn't be delayed or satiated. He bent down and captured her breast in his mouth, curling his stiff tongue over the erect nipple until she cried out in a mix of pleasure and pain. He could make her come with his mouth, his hands, but he also knew the sensations would not be enough. For either of them.

But they'd have to suffice.

"I'm going to buy a whole carton of condoms on my way home," he promised, dropping to his knees.

She braced her hands on the tile and moaned her agreement. With the hiss of the steaming water, he almost didn't hear the words uttered by an accented male voice, followed by the slap of a foil-wrapped packet tossed onto the wet marble floor.

"Don't be stupid, *mon ami*. Take one of mine."

13

"ARMAND?"

Danielle blinked, shook her head to clear the effects of Nick's sensual assault, and then wiped away a circle of steam and looked again through the glass wall. Nick had shot to his feet and was halfway out of the shower with his fists clenched when Danielle grabbed him by his slippery arm.

"Don't! Nick, this is Armand!"

Bad timing or not, Danielle hadn't seen Armand in person since she'd left Paris. Despite his despicably rude interruption and her naked state, she couldn't contain her need to welcome her friend with open arms. He had, after all, come all the way from France.

He held a towel out wide, wrapping her completely and modestly, not that there was much point, before taking her into his embrace.

"These clothes are worth more than you, *ma petite*," he warned, holding her gingerly. "Don't ruin the wool."

"You're such a freakin' dandy," she replied, punching him lightly on the shoulder.

In response, he hugged her tighter and lifted her off the ground. She reacted with a delighted squeal—until Nick cleared his throat.

Armand put her down, then eyed Nick, nude and wet and furious, with an unimpressed expression. For the first time, Danielle realized that Armand reminded her a lot of her brother. She grabbed the towel tighter.

"So, I take it this is your pirate," Armand commented, apparently not entirely approving.

Nick turned his angry gaze on her.

She shrugged and tucked the towel securely between her breasts. "When I first met you, you reminded me of a pirate," she admitted to Nick, not the least bit apologetically. She completely understood his anger toward Armand for interrupting their shower; but she wouldn't apologize for dishing with a friend. But the taut tension between the two men warned her not to ignore the situation in favor of her own stubbornness.

"Besides, it's a very sexy image, if you think about it," she said, sauntering to Nick, who still hadn't covered himself. And he looked magnificent, even wet. Especially wet.

If this was a showdown, Danielle knew Nick would win. She would always love Armand, but Nick owned a piece of her she'd only now begun to understand. She could no more deny their connection than she could ignore that during their lovemaking earlier, she'd caught a glimpse of Sofia's memories, without the magical perfume bottle to influence her. A piece of his lost love existed inside her, and she had no intention of hiding it any longer. But she wasn't admitting it freely, either. Not until she was sure where this relationship was going—and Armand's surprise presence wasn't going to help her find out, particularly if the two men killed each other before she could stop them.

"Who is this man?" Nick asked, his voice quiet, but by no means subtle. An underlying threat rode on each word, a warning Danielle couldn't ignore.

She grabbed a second towel and handed it to Nick. When he didn't make a move to cover himself, his gaze still locked in mortal combat with Armand's, she unfolded the towel and wrapped it around his waist herself.

"Nick Davis, this is Armand Rousseau, a very good friend of mine from Paris."

"From your rehabilitation?" Nick asked, clearly attempting to calm down, but not succeeding.

"No," Armand interrupted. "I met Danielle after her rehabilitation. I was her art instructor, and then her lover. But I don't suppose you wanted to hear that."

Nick stepped around Danielle, his hand protectively on her waist. She couldn't help but roll her eyes. *Men.* Everything was a battle for them. She expected as much from Nick, who possessed an old soul that fed off basic protective instincts, but Armand knew better. He was, as the saying went, a lover, not a fighter.

Surprisingly, Nick answered in a measured, reasonable tone. "You're a piece of Danielle's past. I'm not threatened by you, if that's what you think."

Armand smiled and threw up his hands. "Good! I suppose I should have quietly left when I realized what I was interrupting, but well, *bon jugement* isn't exactly what I'm best known for."

With a careless shrug, Armand left the bathroom.

"Why is he here?" Nick demanded once they were alone.

"I haven't exactly had a chance to ask him, now

have I? And I don't think we're going to find out in here."

Nick eyed the doorway to the VIP room with suspicion. "I don't like him."

Danielle huffed. "You don't know him! Armand is a creative genius and a gentle soul. He helped me work out some of my toughest issues. In fact," she said, growing annoyed, using all her self-control to keep from poking him in his incredibly muscled chest, "it's safe to say that if not for my affair and friendship with Armand, I never would have had the guts to call you over here tonight or order the paints from the Divines or join you in the shower. I was a mess, Nick. Armand helped me through it. If you're jealous, get over it."

Oh, the man could infuriate her faster than anyone else she'd ever met. Nick had found an instantaneous way of creeping under her skin—no, deeper. Little by little, she believed that even before she'd met him, he'd owned a piece of her soul. What would be the consequences of such an intimate connection now that they were lovers? Just because they'd been married in a previous life didn't mean they could make the commitment work in the present.

She grabbed her clothes and marched into the VIP room to dress. She found Armand sitting on the bed, two jars of edible paint in his palm.

"I see you finally got over your aversion to intimate artistry," he teased.

She jabbed her finger in his direction. "You, put those down and shut up. How did you get in here, anyway?"

She dropped her towel and proceeded to wrangle her

damp body back into her bra and panties, unashamed and uncaring of his wounded expression.

He shrugged her ire away. "The guards didn't want to let me in," he explained, having the wisdom to turn his eyes in another direction. "But I can be very persuasive. Besides, I told them I was your brother."

Danielle hopped into her jeans. "And they believed you? In that jacket?"

He waved away her criticism, as well he should. Armand's eye for fashion rivaled his talent with art. Still, her brother, who she guessed had never spent less than a thousand dollars on a shirt, would never have been caught dead in anything so blatantly *haute couture*.

"Tell me about your pirate," he said, tossing the paints aside. He sniffed a leftover smear of Guilty Grape on his hand, then intrigued, swiped a lick. He made a sound of approval

"I'd rather talk about you, frankly," Nick said, marching into the room.

"Me?" Armand asked, complete innocence in his expression. "What a boring topic. I can tell you everything you need to know about me in all of ten minutes. You, *monsieur,* I suspect, are a much more complicated creature."

Silence reigned, snaring Danielle's attention. Her gaze darted between Nick and Armand as she twisted into her T-shirt, and the tension between the two was nearly palpable. This wasn't just about jealousy, but more.

Nick cleared his throat, then spoke with a measured tone that caused prickles at the back of her neck. "It's late. Danielle, may I take you home?"

She shook her head, confused. Why wouldn't he talk to Armand? Why did she get the distinct impression that the emotions Nick grappled with right now pushed beyond simple jealousy of her former lover? His entire body seemed rigid, from his tense shoulders down to his fisted hands.

She glanced at her watch. "The train is still running, or we can hail a cab. Armand, you didn't book a hotel room, did you?"

"Me? I love what little money I have, *ma petite.*" He scooted off the bed and retrieved the hanging bag he'd tossed over a ladder in the corner near the door. "I also remember that you told me your future sister-in-law moved out of her apartment downstairs from you to live with your brother. I figured there would be a spare bed, just for me."

That last part was entirely for Nick's benefit, but Danielle had had too rough of a day to feel grateful. If she went that far, she'd also have to acknowledge that Nick had some sort of hold on her, some tie akin to commitment—and that simply wasn't the case. Maybe she was starting to believe that she and Nick might have been lovers, maybe even husband and wife, in a previous life. But that wasn't the scenario now, was it?

"That apartment hasn't been rented yet. I'm sure you could stay there tonight." She grabbed her tote bag, then realizing she couldn't just leave Nick without attempting an explanation, she asked Armand to meet her at the door.

He waved at Nick, then did as she asked. When they were alone, she hoped the fury she witnessed, kept so carefully in check, wasn't directed at her.

"I'm sorry about Armand walking in," she said, forcing a smile. "He really has no shame at all."

Nick nodded. "You weren't embarrassed?"

"With Armand?" She closed the distance between her and Nick, marveling at how a few feet seemed like an insurmountable chasm when he appeared so perturbed. She supposed she should have exhibited some shame at having someone walk in on her and Nick at such an intimate moment, but the truth was, it wasn't just any someone—it was Armand. The man had seen her naked from several different angles and an extremely close proximity. They'd had phone sex just a couple of days ago! She wondered what Nick would think if she admitted that the last sexual encounter she'd had with Armand had been all Nick's fault.

She decided to keep that tidbit to herself. "Armand got me through one of the toughest times in my life, Nick. I went through rehab and got clean, but I was still…damaged. Guys would look at me, you know, like they were interested, and I'd just recoil. After what I'd been through on the streets…"

Her voice trailed off. She didn't want to tell him the whole sordid truth, not because she thought he'd think less of her, but because she didn't want to relive the violence and ugliness again. Healing hadn't been easy, but she'd moved beyond that pain and she had no desire to reopen the wounds.

"Armand was very patient and gentle and sweet. And outrageous and fun and irrepressible! You can't know how he changed my life, how he made me realize that having sex again, *enjoying* sex again—even after what I'd been through—was okay."

Nick's lips flattened into a grim line. "And you love him for this?"

"Of course I love him!" She threw her hands in the air, wondering how any man could be so dense. Then she remembered. He was a man. He was territorial. It was a natural reaction and not entirely unwarranted. "But not how you think," she assured him, touching his arm lightly. "Armand and I *were* lovers, I won't deny that. But now, we're really just great friends. Nick, you have to accept that, because I can't change the past anymore than you can."

His breath still rushed with carefully checked hostility but at least he was listening. "Danielle, I can't make an accusation against a man I've known for five minutes, but I'd feel better if Armand stayed at a hotel."

She pursed her lips, but with a smile. "What's this really about, Nick?"

"Not jealousy."

From the intensity in his eyes, she believed him. But she still wasn't about to send her good friend to a hotel when he could stay in the extra apartment below hers. "I can't do that, Nick. He's my friend and I trust him. I can also take care of myself. You're going to have to make a choice. Start a fight with me that you won't win, or leave me with a hot, sexy kiss that will whet my appetite for you and you alone."

After a moment's hesitation, he chose the latter. Danielle concentrated completely on the feel of his mouth on hers, the intoxicating quality of his taste. She wished she could invite Nick home with her, but she sensed the animosity between Armand and Nick needed at least one night to cool. She'd repair the damage of Armand's interruption tomorrow.

When he broke away from her, he cupped her chin in his palm. "Promise me you'll be careful."

"With Armand?" she asked, shocked. The idea of Armand hurting her was too ridiculous to comprehend.

Nick shook his head. "No, not just with Armand. With making it home. I know there is no evidence that the scaffolding accident and the fire were directed at you personally, and I know that you are tough and streetwise and perfectly capable of protecting yourself, but I'm still asking you, please, to show a little extra caution."

She slipped into his arms and a blanket of warmth enveloped her at his heartfelt embrace. He cared about her. And not once tonight had he asked her if she remembered anything about Sofia. She had remembered, but he hadn't asked—did this mean he valued her just as much as her connection to his former wife? And though he clearly wasn't thrilled about Armand's surprise visit, he also cared enough about her not to let her former lover's presence get in the way of their…what? Relationship? Affair?

She didn't know and at the moment, she was too tired to care. With one long, lingering kiss, they said goodbye for the night. With a whisper against her ear, he promised to call her first thing in the morning, and she didn't doubt for one minute that he would keep his word.

Nick lingered behind, promising to lock up the VIP room and clear away all the evidence of their tryst—and have a serious talking to with the security guards who had believed Armand's claim that he was Sebastian Stone. Part of her hated allowing him to handle the situation when it was her responsibility, but the other, less stubborn part appreciated the break. She was too tired to reprimand anyone. She just wanted to go home.

Danielle found Armand near the front door, where the hostess stand to the restaurant would be placed once the renovations were complete. Nearby, a pile of two-by-fours and several sacks of grout separated them from where the scaffolding had fallen.

"Ahead of schedule, you say?" he asked, eyeing the destruction.

She grabbed him by the sleeve and led him out of the building. "A lot can change in forty-eight hours. Why didn't you tell me your were coming to Chicago?"

He sighed with audible frustration. "Does the term *surprise* mean anything to you? You remember that gallery in New York I told you about? The owner has been after me to come to the States for years, to consider a show. When I heard that peculiar sound in your voice the other night," he said, capturing her hand as they bounded down the steps, "I decided it was time for you and I to have a face-to-face. I thought I could help convince you to pursue your pirate. Apparently, you've done *très bien* on your own."

Danielle smiled and remained silent, watching for a taxi as a spate of cars roared by them. She yawned, the exhaustion from the past two days catching up to her. Luckily, a few minutes later, an empty yellow cab swerved up to the curb before Armand could say anything more about her love life. He might not understand discretion when in private, but he would remain silent in the company of the taxi driver.

Only Armand would fly across an ocean to help her get laid. She took his hand, twining her fingers with his as they sped through Chicago on the way to her apartment. Lights flashed across Armand's aristocratic face, reminding her of how handsome and bohemian-looking he was. Long, iron-straight hair, lengthier than Nick's, but pulled back similarly in a ponytail. A proud, narrow nose and generous, naturally pouting lips. Quick, intelligent eyes in rich espresso-brown, lighter than Nick's but not half as soulful. Then she remembered how Armand had swept her off her feet so easily in Paris. Who wouldn't fall for a god like him? The infatuation and lust between them had been powerful and incontrovertible. But she'd learned from him that strong emotions like desire and need didn't last without a strong foundation beneath them. Ultimately, they'd wanted such different things from life. She'd wanted to return to the States, build a relationship with her brother, find a career or calling that would prove her to be a productive, capable woman rather than a needful addict. Armand's goal had been and still was simple—he wanted to paint and make just enough money from his art and his teaching to provide himself with expensive clothes and fine wines. He wanted to take lovers. Have fun and bear no responsibility to anyone. He had already established an ideal life for himself—the kind where he could hop on a plane without a moment's notice and go crash with a friend.

But seeing her former lover again brought a question

to her mind that she wasn't prepared to answer. Did she and Nick have anything remotely solid enough to support the relationship looming over them? What did Nick want from life? He had his carpentry, but she knew from when she hired him that his business was new. He was, after all, a gypsy. Would he stay put long enough to explore their connection completely, or would his instinctual wanderlust make that impossible?

"You look confused," Armand said softly as the taxi turned onto her street. "And exhausted."

She laughed from the pure understatement. "You have no idea."

"The pirate?" he asked.

"He's a gypsy," she corrected.

Armand scooted closer to her and wrapped his arm over her shoulder. "*Même différence.* He's sensual and strong and probably won't stay very long. Why is this a problem?"

Danielle dug into her bag and pulled out her wallet, paying the fare and tipping the driver generously. As expected, Armand launched into a rant, entirely in French, on how she was squandering her money now that she had it. She smiled all the way up to the front door. She'd managed to deflect Armand's last question, because frankly, she wasn't sure she'd like the answer—even if she knew what it was.

NICK TOOK THE STAIRS three at a time. By the time he reached Jeta's door, she already had it open.

"You shouldn't open your door at night without knowing who was coming up the stairs," he chastised.

She waved her withered hand at him. "As if I didn't know. Shut the door and sit. What happened?"

"Milosh."

Jeta's eyes grew wide and she lowered herself into the overstuffed chair she'd purchased from a neighbor down the hall. The massive rose chintz recliner nearly swallowed her whole, but Nick saw how her face eased whenever she sat there, the cushions buoying her old bones.

"You saw him?"

Nick sat on the edge of the coffee table, close enough to take her hands in his. "I'm not sure. There are differences. In his height, his body shape, even his hair."

With a frown, Nick realized that perhaps his instant dislike of the man had been based on his male pride rather than his gypsy instincts. Milosh had been a rare blond in their dark and swarthy group. His eyes had been light—blue or green, perhaps—not dark brown. And while he'd been slim, he hadn't been as tall as Armand, who matched Nick inch for inch.

"That means nothing," Jeta claimed. "Eve explained to me about the reincarnation. She said there was no basis for believing that the souls of the dead come back in the same body. Remember, she said some people believe they were once animals."

Nick nodded, somewhat surprised that Jeta had this knowledge. He'd thought she'd ignored his suspicion about Danielle and Sofia and had simply come with him to Chicago because she was family and she couldn't bear to abandon him. He should have known better. Jeta was too intelligent a woman to dive into a complete unknown.

"I don't know, Jeta. The emotions I felt around this man were so strong. Jealousy, anger. I could barely control them."

Jeta smiled. "Is this man interested in your Danielle?"

Nick sniffed. Not according to his words, but the admiration in Armand's eyes when he looked at Danielle was unmistakable. Of course, he couldn't blame the man. He likely looked at her the same way. "They were once lovers."

Jeta's eyebrows disappeared beneath her scarf and then one of her annoyingly all-knowing smiles curved her lips.

"But that's not why I think he's Milosh," he insisted, though his indignation died halfway through the claim. "Is it?"

Jeta shook her head. "I don't know, Nicholai. Did you leave them alone together?"

He bit the inside of his mouth, but the pain didn't lessen the ache of his powerlessness. "I had no choice. They are friends and Danielle is a very stubborn woman. My protests would have gone nowhere and following them would have done no good."

With her cragged fingers, Jeta took Nick's hands in hers. "You did best to come to me before you made wild accusations. If you push her away, all of this would be for nothing. Alexis could tell me nothing more about Milosh than that he was near. Did this lover of Danielle's act with jealousy toward you?"

"Former lover," he corrected her. "No. He didn't seem to care much one way or another that I was in her life. But Milosh never acted with jealousy either. And yet, when he got the chance, he killed her.''

He pushed off from the chair, spearing his hands through his hair. "Damn, I had no proof! But I know Milosh pushed her off that cliff as certainly as I am in this room.''

Jeta nodded, her mouth pursed. It did not matter to his grandmother that they'd never had any evidence with which to accuse Milosh. They'd known. Alexis had not seen it, nor had Jeta been able to conjure a spirit to verify their suspicion, but their hearts had told them the man was guilty. Without proof, they couldn't bring the matter up before the clan's leaders, so they'd suffered in silence.

Milosh had not been so charitable. He'd done all he could to intimate to the clan leaders that Nicholai, in a jealous rage, had taken his wife to the cliff and pushed her off, then returned to the camp and pretended innocence. Milosh had been with the group of men who'd discovered the scarf near the ledge. And Nicholai had, on more than one occasion, taken one or two of his bachelor clansmen to task for looking at his wife with stares that lasted too long or possessed the slightest hint of lust. He'd only been protecting what was his—but Milosh had used his territorial actions against him.

When the clan leaders had remained unconvinced, Milosh had taken a step that had shocked everyone who knew him—and had sealed Nicholai's belief that he'd murdered Sofia himself. He'd gone to the *gaujo* police. He'd reported the disappearance of his wife's cousin and pointed the finger at Nicholai. Unable to fight a force of armed men who'd relished the idea of hanging a gypsy—guilty or not—Nicholai, Alexis and Jeta had left the clan. And France.

So long ago, Nick thought. And now the cycle of life had brought them back to this same emotional spot. Unlike with Danielle, it wasn't his instincts drawing him to the conclusion that reincarnation was at play. It was his head. Armand was from France. He'd shown up unannounced just as Nick had made strides in convincing Danielle of who she'd once been. The man's emotional ties to his former lover were incredibly strong. Had Nick made a huge mistake in allowing Armand to take Danielle home? Had he somehow condemned his lover into the hands of a killer? Again?

Or was he simply envious of the relationship Danielle shared with a man who'd helped her heal?

He couldn't live with not knowing the answer. Not even for one night. He knew Danielle wanted nothing more than to be respected for her strength and intelligence, but he had to check and make sure she wasn't in danger.

"I've got to go," Nick said, standing. He stopped when he reached the door. "Do you need anything?"

Jeta grinned. "I'm fine, Nicholai. You needn't worry about me. I am a gypsy. I acclimate to my surroundings. You do what you must."

He dashed back to his grandmother, kissed her cheek, then disappeared out the door and down the hall. He was no fool—he would not rush in with accusations or wild claims when, in truth, he had nothing more than a sketchily drawn conclusion that Armand Rousseau was not who he seemed to be.

But he'd find out. Tonight.

14

"THAT'S IT? That's the whole story?"

Armand looked at her with his mouth hanging open. If she told him one more thing, she suspected he might collapse from shock. She'd dumped a hell of a lot on him in the past hour and since he was desperately trying to believe everything she said, he clearly couldn't take another word about reincarnation, magic, gypsies and murder. Luckily, she was done. From her first meeting with Nick in her office, to the legend of the perfume bottle and their unbelievable encounter in his loft at his warehouse, she'd told him everything she knew. She'd confessed to Armand that Nick believed she was the reincarnated soul of his dead wife, Sofia, who'd likely been murdered by a jealous rival. And most surprising of all—she'd admitted that she believed him.

"Except for the weird things happening at the restaurant, I think I've about covered it."

She fell into her overstuffed beanbag chair, completely exhausted. Pouring out her soul, even to a man she knew she could trust, had sapped the last bit of her depleted energy. She blinked, and could have sworn she heard her eyelids scrape over her moistureless eyes.

"What happened at the restaurant?" he asked.

"This morning, we discovered that someone had set approximately ten blowtorches at the base of our scaffolding, melting the bars and knocking it to the ground."

Armand's face skewed in disgust. "Was anyone hurt?"

"No," she answered, breathing another sigh of relief. "It happened when no one was on the site. Then tonight, even with the increased security I hired, someone set a fire in a garbage bin out back. Again, nothing serious happened, but it could have. It's been a hot, dry summer and most of our materials are highly flammable."

"You called the police?"

"Of course. They think it's just vandals. Apparently, this sort of thing happens on construction sites all the time."

"But you don't think so?"

Danielle sat up and forced her eyes open wide. The sting sent jabs of pain to her entire face. God, she wanted to sleep.

"No, Armand, I don't. Like Nick said to me tonight, I have an uneasy feeling."

"You were worried about your competitors before, no? Do you suspect them?"

She shook her head, uncertain. She'd forgotten that she'd discussed her business problems with Armand again, after the fake inspector had tried to enter the restaurant, either to steal their concept or report back to competitors. That scenario didn't seem so outrageous, but vandalized scaffolding and arson did seem more like the actions of angry kids rather than monied professionals. And yet, she had a strong hunch that more was at play—perhaps because none of the mishaps had happened until she'd announced to the investors that the project was on time and on budget.

Was Nick right? Was someone trying to hurt her? Not physically, but professionally?

"Competitors wouldn't act so amateurishly, I'm sure of it." She shifted in the beanbag. Not even the notoriously comfortable stuffed chair could quite cushion her aching, exhausted muscles. "But that's not even my biggest worry, Armand. What am I supposed to do with the knowledge that somewhere inside me, somewhere that is growing closer and closer to the surface, I might be this Sofia Vaux, this gypsy woman whose face I can see just as I see my own?"

"Wait!" Armand said, scurrying from the couch to her beanbag so quickly, he'd practically flown. "You've seen her?"

"I did. Tonight. In a mirror. My face, but clearly, hers, too. And Nick was there."

"You experienced one of her memories without the bottle?"

Had she really left that part out? Not surprising since the brief glimpse, experienced amid the euphoria of an amazing orgasm, had hardly seemed real at the time. She'd tried to explain the flash away, or at least, push the experience to the back of her mind until she had the time to process it. But she didn't have that luxury. Not now that she'd brought Armand up to speed on her story.

"When Nick and I made love tonight, I saw myself—no, Sofia—looking in the mirror. But it was a small mirror, the kind a woman keeps on her dresser, with a handle. Old, chipped, but valued, not for its price, but sentimentally. I'm almost sure it belonged to Sofia's mother. The silver part was faded around the edges. But the woman in the reflection was me, Armand. I could feel the truth. And behind me, I saw Nick.''

Armand shook his head, as if he didn't want to believe any more of the amazing things she'd told him so far. She half expected him to accuse her of being on drugs again, but the topic hadn't come up. And she knew that if Armand suspected she was high, he'd cart her off to the nearest rehab center available, even if it cost him the last euro in his pocket. No, her friend with the limitless imagination and creatively open mind simply believed her—just like she'd prayed he would.

His eyes, dark with seriousness, bored into hers. "You're sure this was a flash from the past?"

She nodded. She had no doubt. The moment the woman in her memory, the moment Sofia had caught sight of Nicholai, she'd been overcome with emotion. Just like the night at the pond. Pure, concentrated love—and nothing else. No insecurity. No doubts. Knowing how Danielle felt about Nick in the present, she knew the vision had been from the past. Yes, in the here and now she cared for Nick deeply. But a woman like her didn't jump into any relationship without insecurities and doubts. They may not have been a part of the woman she was then, but they most certainly drove who she was now.

"*Ma petite,*" Armand said, laying his hand gently over hers. "This is outrageous. The fact that I believe you is even more insane. I mean, I've always believed that magic exists, that there are things our puny mortal minds cannot completely understand, but I never thought I'd know someone…''

His voice trailed off, giving Danielle the second she needed to rest. She closed her eyes again and by the time she had the strength to pull her lids up, she heard angry voices in the hallway.

Angry male voices.

Had she fallen asleep? She looked around her apartment and realized the lights had all been turned off and someone, no doubt Armand, had spread a blanket over her. Now, she could hear him arguing, in French, with someone in the hall.

Not just any someone, either.

His deep, melodic voice had sent shivers up her spine since the first day they'd met.

Nick.

She crawled to her feet, her balance thrown off by her extreme exhaustion and her odd position in the beanbag. Her foot was asleep so she clumsily ambled to the door. After yanking it open, she interrupted the barely hushed shouting match. ''Can't a girl get any rest around here?''

''I was trying, *ma petite*,'' Armand spat, ''but this *gitan fou* insists on seeing for himself that you are safe and sound.''

Nick pushed Armand out of the way and grabbed Danielle by the arms. His grip smarted, and when she winced, he immediately let her go.

''Danielle, are you all right?''

She rubbed her arms, concentrating on where his

hands had wrapped around her like two vise grips. He was spooked, and she would bet the entire restaurant it wasn't simple jealousy.

"I'm fine, Nick. Bruised now, but fine. And tired. Really, really tired."

He reached out, but as he had when they'd first met and interacted, he resisted touching her. And despite the pain he'd inflicted a few seconds ago, she wasn't pleased that he was holding back. She ached for his caress. Craved it.

"I'm sorry," he whispered. "I'm just very afraid for you."

She understood, though she wasn't sure why. Was this cosmic connection filling in gaps between them she'd never thought she'd fill? Just having him near calmed her, cleared her mind. Her smile was tiny, but genuine.

"Come inside. Both of you. We'll talk."

Nick shook his head. "No, no more talking, Danielle. I won't have you in danger one minute more."

He spun toward Armand, rage narrowing his eyes. "I know this man is your friend, but I suspect his appearance here in Chicago is no accident."

Armand rolled his eyes. "Of course it's not an accident! I came to help the two of you get together. *Certains hommes sont de tels idiots!*"

Nick didn't move. "I don't believe you."

Danielle stamped her foot and turned on her heel, heading back into the apartment. Okay, on some level, this jealousy thing was kind of cute and very flattering. But on every other level, including the one closest to the surface of her worn patience, it was completely pissing her off.

She turned, thinking to slam the door on both of them, but Nick blocked her.

"Please, Danielle, this isn't what you think."

"Then what is it?"

Nick hesitated for a split second, and that was all the motivation she needed to leave him standing there. She didn't have the energy for anything more.

"Wait!"

She pulled in a deep breath and faced him. "You'd better tell me fast, Nick, or I'm going to bed. My brain is swimming with magic and reincarnated spirits and fires and failure...I just can't deal with much anymore, do you understand?"

"Your friend Armand may be the man who killed you."

Both she and Armand shouted a disbelieving "What?"

"That's absurd!" Armand protested. "How dare you! You've met me once, have known me for all of twenty minutes and you accuse me of wanting to harm Danielle? *Êtes-vous fou?*"

"No, I'm not insane," Nick insisted, though for a moment, Danielle saw a flash across his eyes that told her he wasn't so sure.

A sudden rush, warm and liquid, flowed through her, zapping her from the inside out. An ache haunted her chest, then settled into the pit of her stomach, heavy and hot. She crossed the distance between her and Nick and grabbed his hand. His flesh was cool, almost clammy. She couldn't resist pressing his palm to her breast, encased in her hands, to give him warmth.

She turned to look at her friend. "Armand, please. I understand you are insulted, but this isn't an ordinary situation. Can you wait outside? For just a minute?"

He cursed colorfully in French, but did what she asked, slamming the door behind him.

"What's going on, Nick?"

"I've asked you to trust me about so much, I don't know how I can ask you again."

"You just ask."

His eyes widened. "You believe me, don't you?"

"About me? Yes, Nick. I believe you. I don't know how much of all of this is real, but I do feel Sofia inside me. A piece of her, anyway."

His entire body tensed. She knew he wanted to hold her. She could see the desperation in his eyes. He ground his teeth in his effort to keep her at a safe distance. But for whom? For him? Or for her?

"What do you feel?" he asked.

A tiny grin played on her lips, no matter how she tried to tamp it down. "I feel her love. Not for some man you were in a previous life, either. For you. Nicholai Vaux, the gypsy."

He stepped back, but she didn't release his hand. She hadn't realized until the words left her lips that she'd stumbled onto something shocking. Perhaps, even, unbelievable.

"There's more to this story, isn't there?" she asked.

"Yes," he answered quickly. "But if you can believe me, it's more outrageous than what I've told you so far, including my claim about Armand."

She nodded, understanding that perhaps now was not the time to delve into whatever last secret Nick was keeping from her, the one that somehow explained why his soul felt so very old to her, why Sofia's love, so alive inside her now, seemed focused not on the man her lover had become in a new life, but on Nicholai himself. As if Nick wasn't a reincarnation of Sofia's husband—but that he was the man she'd made love to on the bank of the pond, the man she'd looked at in the mirror with such unadulterated devotion.

"Tell me more about Armand."

Nick released a pent-up breath, then pulled Danielle to the couch. They sat, hands entwined. "You have to know that I didn't come to Chicago alone. My grandmother came with me. Her name is Jeta. She and my cousin, Alexis, are the only family I have left."

"Where's Alexis?"

"In Atlanta. She didn't believe in my quest to find you, to discover if you were, somehow, Sofia. She and Sofia were very close. I think the concept was too difficult for her to face."

"I know how she feels," she cracked.

Nick rewarded her humor with a smile. "Yes, well, you have to understand that Alexis has a special talent. A gift for Sight."

Danielle squinted and pulled back, not sure she understood. "Sight? You mean, she can see the future?"

Nick nodded his head. "I'm not sure how it works, but Alexis has had visions of future events for her entire life. And yesterday, she contacted Jeta. She said she saw Milosh. Here. Nearby. He is a dangerous man, Danielle."

"Who is Milosh?"

"The man who I suspect killed my Sofia. The man who pushed her over that cliff in France."

Danielle suddenly knew, not from her own memory, but from bits and pieces of what Nick had told her so far. "He's the one she was supposed to have married. The one who married her cousin instead."

"Yes," Nick verified. "Alexis sees him here, with us."

"And just because Armand is French, looks like a gypsy and is my former lover, you suspect he may be this Milosh? Or that he is a reincarnation of Milosh?"

Nick didn't know how else to explain this. He wished he were more certain about his suspicion, but the truth was, he'd only tonight given Alexis's prediction any real credence. Armand's sudden and unexplainable entrance into their lives had gone beyond coincidence in his mind. Either Armand was Milosh, or else he had impeccably bad timing.

"I don't know, Danielle. But I do know that when I learned about reincarnation, I studied a theory that said that when the spirit is looking to work out conflicts from the past, the other spirits tied together by that conflict often find ways to reunite. Even coming from different countries or speaking different languages doesn't stop them."

"Like some sort of weird cosmic spawning?"

Nick had no idea what she was talking about.

"Like salmon? The fish? No matter where in the rivers they are, when the instinct to mate and lay eggs hits them, they automatically gravitate back to the place they were spawned, so they can do the same. You're saying that the spirits of Sofia, Nicholai and Milosh are inextricably tied. That no matter what lifetime we're in, at some point, we'll come together and work through our conflict again.''

Nick breathed a quick sigh of relief. She understood. Good. But that didn't make his claim any less outrageous.

''If that's the case, why doesn't Armand know? If he is Milosh, wouldn't he know?''

''You didn't acknowledge the presence of Sofia in you until tonight. Even after I showed you the visions with the perfume bottle, you still doubted.''

''Does Armand look like Milosh?''

Nick pursed his lips. ''No. But I'm not sure that physical form is a requirement. That you look exactly like Sofia could be a quirk of fate, a means by which I could find you again. But Milosh could be anyone.''

''Then why do you suspect Armand? Because he was my lover?''

Nick nodded. He couldn't deny the truth, or the timing. He'd been thrown off by the accidents at the restaurant site, then tonight, while talking to Jeta, realized those could have been entirely unrelated. Or not. He simply wasn't sure.

''I want to find out for sure,'' he admitted.

''Why? So you can hurt Armand? I won't allow that, Nick. Not under any circumstances.''

''No, that's just it. This may be our chance to settle that conflict. If Armand is Milosh, then we can make peace, don't you see? End that cycle of anger and jealousy. It has to be this way, I think. Or else, why would fate bring you back to me?''

In a rush of passion Nick could no longer control, he slipped his hand around Danielle's neck and pulled her lips to his. Their kiss was desperate, intense and needful. He paid attention to every aspect of her taste, every texture, every degree of heat. He wanted nothing more than to spend the rest of the night right here on this couch, touching her, pleasuring her, branding her with the love they'd shared a century ago, but he knew they had to settle this score before they could move on.

Danielle pulled away, her eyes glazed with desire. She blinked the dreamy quality away and set her expression with complete determination.

"Okay, then we don't have any choice, do we? We need to settle this, once and for all."

He nodded.

Danielle jumped to her feet. "Then let's do it. The bottle can prove to Armand who he is, or who he isn't, right?"

Nick stood and took her hand, unwilling to let her go again, even for a moment. How she'd grown to trust him after he'd handed her unbelievable story after unbelievable story astonished him, made him wonder how he could have deserved such an amazing woman, not once in his life, but twice.

"I believe the bottle can help us, if your friend is game."

She threw back her head and laughed. "Armand? Game is practically his middle name."

15

AS SHE'D PREDICTED TO NICK, Armand had been nearly giddy with excitement after she'd fully disclosed Nick's suspicions about his supernatural ties to her. His legendary affectation of ennui, the key to the sophisticated persona he presented to the world, vanished. Unlike her brother, Sebastian, who really was disenchanted and worldly, Armand possessed an irrepressible spirit, keen for adventure and sparked by the unknown. He'd chattered nonstop the entire ride to the warehouse in Nick's truck, wondering aloud how he could have been so stupid not to have figured out this connection before. He'd always wondered why he and Danielle had not only connected so quickly as lovers, but how they'd maintained a friendship from separate countries. He'd constantly questioned the empty feeling he'd experienced since Danielle had left. He would have maybe thought he'd been in love, until he realized how absurd that was. Now, he had an explanation he could cling to! He was the reincarnated spirit of Milosh, the man Sofia had spurned for Nicholai.

It was all so romantic, Danielle feared he might have a seizure from all the excitement. He barely allowed a word in from either Nick or her, but after a while, Danielle didn't care. She sat beside Nick in the cab of the truck, her hand tucked in his, her head softly pressed to his shoulder, feeling truly relaxed for the first time in days.

With the short snippet of sleep she'd stolen in her apartment, she'd gained the insight she needed to put this all into perspective. Whether or not Sofia or her memories still existed inside Danielle didn't really matter. Yes, knowing she possessed the same spirit of a loving, but somewhat delicate gypsy woman did explain so much about her own life—the restlessness, the wandering, the inability ever to feel safe or settled until she'd reconnected with her brother and had met Armand. Of course, with his soul possibly connected to hers cosmically, she now also understood why they'd bonded so fast and why he'd been able to help her heal so many of her past wounds. And, of course, why they hadn't been destined to be anything more than friends. She didn't particularly like the idea that he might have killed her in another life, but if reincarnation was a mode for fixing mistakes, she figured he'd already made up for that one murderous past-life transgression.

She also found comfort in knowing that her instantaneous lust for Nick had been more than just physical. Although, she thought with a naughty smile, the physical part was a particularly yummy perk.

What was important was that fate had somehow seen clear to give them a second chance. And knowing just how sweet a second chance at life could be, she couldn't allow this opportunity for love to pass her by.

There was much about Nick to love, she realized. He was romantic and patient, sensual and careful. He weighed his words and took great care that he didn't ask for more than he would give himself. He showed his deep ability to care in his art, his carvings. And as much as she supposed feminists would blanch at this admission, she liked the way he wanted to take care of her, all the while acknowledging that she had the capacity to take care of herself.

From the first night in his loft, she'd wondered why he didn't hold her violent, drugged-out past against her, but now she understood. In the great scheme of life, her brief five years on the streets were a blip in time. Today, tonight, mattered so much more.

Nick pulled up to the curb in front of the warehouse. The minute he doused the headlights, Danielle felt a chill rush over her skin. The street was dark. Really, really dark. She'd been here last night, so she knew something wasn't normal.

Nick leaned forward and peered out the front window. "The streetlight is out. That's weird. It was fine, earlier."

Armand had already unbuckled his seat belt and was pushing out of the truck's cab. "Lends an air of ambience, doesn't it? We're about to toy with the mysteries of the paranormal—it should be dark and creepy."

Danielle laughed at Armand's French-accented Bela Lugosi imitation. At least he was keeping his sense of humor about this whole mad escapade.

Nick got out and Danielle after him. For a brief instant, she leaned fully against him, stirring passions that were very much a part of the here and now. "Let's just get inside. I want to settle this. Until we deal with what might have happened in the past, we can't face the truth about the present.''

Nick grinned and the expression was enough to make her sigh. They jogged to the curb hand in hand, but both froze when they spotted the door to the warehouse—slightly ajar.

''Is someone inside?'' she asked.

Nick held up his hand, pushing Danielle toward Armand with clear reluctance. ''Stay here.''

Danielle smirked. ''As if.''

Nick huffed his impatience. ''It might just have been Jeta. She often stops by, brings me food and she might not have locked the door.'' He turned to Danielle, ''I suppose I should admit now that I'm a lousy cook.''

She slapped her hand over her mouth to keep from laughing. ''Good. I'd hate to think you were better than me at something so domestic.''

Nick dug into his pocket and pulled out fifty cents. He slapped the coins into Armand's hand, then pointed down the street. ''There is a pay phone at the end of the block. Dial 911.''

Danielle reached for her cell, but realized she hadn't brought her bag. Still, when Armand turned to follow Nick's directive, she caught him by the arm. ''There's a bar right across the street. It's closer.''

''It's got to be closed for the night,'' Nick said.

Danielle shook her head. She knew this neighborhood and had spent quite a bit of time loitering on this very block. The bar across the street didn't officially close until after 4:00 a.m., even though the crowds disappeared around two. ''The owner doesn't close for another fifteen minutes. Go, Armand, and stay put until the police arrive.''

"And you?"

"I'm going with Nick."

They both opened their mouths to protest, but she managed to silence them with a glare. "I'm an expert at staying out of the way, believe me. But if someone is inside the warehouse, they might be after valuables, and that includes the bottle. You remember, the bottle we need to settle all this once and for all?''

Armand silently crossed the deserted street, disappearing behind the door to the bar. Nick locked his fists onto his hips, his gaze intense. She figured he was weighing his options. To argue or not to argue? She made the choice for him by marching toward the entrance.

She turned before she opened the door. "If someone is robbing the place, it isn't a great idea to surprise them.''

Nick squeezed in front of her. She backed up, giving him the lead. This was, after all, his home and workplace.

"I've been robbed once before. Some guys pawing around for food. We'll just sneak in quietly and check out what's going on. If anyone is still inside, and if they look dangerous or drugged out, we'll come back out until the police arrive.''

Nick pulled the door open just enough for them to slip inside the lobby. An old, abandoned reception desk sat like a stark sentinel in front of the main doors leading to the warehouse. There was a light on inside, but no noise.

"Maybe they've already come and gone," Danielle suggested, keeping her voice low.

Nick nodded as he continued to move forward. She couldn't blame him for wanting to protect the perfume bottle, which was likely priceless not only because of its age and history, but the artistry of the silver work and crystal. He also had his tools to worry about, and the beds. If someone vandalized the work he'd already done, the restaurant would never open on time—at least, not with the hand-carved centerpieces he'd worked so hard to produce.

They entered the main warehouse, sliding behind a shelf and then prowling deeper into the room, using the rows of shelving to block their movements from anyone who might be on the other side. Peering through breaks in the metal racks, they could see Nick's toolbox, upturned and empty. The hand-sized power tools he'd kept on the main bench were gone. But the bed frame he'd been working on, clamped in a vise and not yet assembled, looked completely untouched. Anyone could have broken in simply to steal what they could to buy drugs or booze or food. And the thieves could be long gone by now.

They still heard nothing. No one rooting around. Nothing being dropped, no voices. The place seemed completely empty, but with the loft so far away, they couldn't be sure. They did, however, have a clear view of the staircase.

Nick turned to her, holding both of her arms firmly. "Go outside and wait for the police," he whispered. "If the authorities show up, they might mistake us for thieves. So you should go. But I want to wait here, in case someone comes down from the loft.''

"The only thing up there of value is the perfume bottle," she reminded him.

Nick's mouth was a grim line. ''They'll only find it if they know where to look. I didn't leave it sitting out.''

She smiled. Of course, he didn't. He might be from another time and place, but he certainly wasn't stupid.

On her way out of the building, Danielle nearly ran into Armand in the lobby.

"American police!" Armand complained, his voice barely hushed. ''They promised to send someone, but said you shouldn't have gone inside. I came to tell you to stay out until they arrived, but they didn't seem to be in much of a hurry.''

Danielle patted his shoulder to calm him down, then led him outside. ''A possible robbery doesn't take priority over other crimes, Armand. Nick doesn't think anyone else is still inside, and I agree with him. Some valuable tools are gone, and that's probably it.''

"The bottle?" Armand asked, gripping her hand tightly.

She shook her head. ''We don't know yet.''

After five fruitless minutes waiting for the police, who Danielle now believed weren't going to make an appearance anytime soon, they finally abandoned the wait. Nick called to them from the loft, his voice no longer hushed.

"There's no one up here."

"Did they take anything?" Danielle asked.

Nick frowned. ''My favorite wines, but that's it.''

"What about the bottle?" Armand called.

Nick grinned and held up the carved wooden box. Danielle grabbed Armand by the hand and yanked him upstairs behind her. When they rounded the landing, Nick had placed the case on the coffee table.

He went around the room lighting lamps and setting the stage. Danielle led Armand to the coffee table, then nodded for him to sit on the cushions on the floor.

"Touching the bottle can be very draining," she warned him. "It's best if you're sitting down."

Armand didn't take his eyes off the casket. "It's inside?"

Danielle silently touched his hand. "I've got to warn you. The experience is really strange. Your eyes will get so heavy, you won't be able to keep them open. You'll experience a sort of tunnel vision, but what's at the end of the tunnel will be from your distant past. If," she emphasized, "you are who Nick thinks you are."

Nick joined them, folding into the space beside Danielle.

"How will I know?" Armand asked.

Nick glanced at Danielle, uncertainty in his eyes. "I'm not sure. The magic in the bottle was created specifically for Danielle. I have to hope that if you are Milosh, touching the bottle will show you a time when he and Sofia were together. Perhaps, all three of us, since we're all here. I don't know. And we won't know until we give this a try."

Nick tugged the box closer to him and unfastened the latch. The atmosphere in the room tensed as they sucked in a collective breath.

When Nick threw back the top, they gasped.

The bottle was gone.

"NICK?"

Nicholai stared at the empty indentation in the scarlet silk, stunned by the absence of the bottle. He'd stashed the casket in a ceiling tile above his bed. He couldn't imagine that anyone would have known where to look.

But he couldn't deny the obvious—the bottle was gone.

"I don't understand," he said. "The casket was in the hiding place. No one knew where I kept it. No one."

Nick's mind raced with possibilities. He'd been in a rush when he'd come back to the loft before heading to Danielle's apartment. He'd come home to the warehouse specifically to make sure the bottle was hidden, but he'd hurried inside with little on his mind except reaching Danielle before Armand did anything to hurt her. He'd been running on pure instinct. Perhaps he'd left the ceiling tile slightly ajar, or had left some other clue that told the thief where to look.

Downstairs, they'd taken valuable tools. Up here, they'd pilfered his wine. He had no reason to believe anyone had specifically come looking for the bottle, but he couldn't be sure.

"What do we do now?" Danielle asked.

Three heads jerked toward the back of the loft at the sound of a slamming door. Not nearby. Above them.

"What's back there?" Danielle asked, scrambling to her feet.

Nick shot up after her, catching her by the hand before she left his sight. "A stairwell to the roof. I've never used it."

Armand pushed past them. "Well, someone's used it tonight and it could be our thief."

Before Nick could stop him, the Frenchman rushed to the door and yanked it open. Nick knew he'd kept it locked from the inside, but the key that had been hanging on a peg nearby was gone. By the time he processed that Armand intended to rush onto the roof and catch the thief red-handed, he'd disappeared up the stairs before Nick could stop him.

But he raced after Danielle, who'd followed Armand. She was urging her friend to stop in a hushed plea. They argued in French, with Armand insisting they had to retrieve the bottle before some drugged-out thug dropped it or broke it. Then they'd never discover the truth. Nick stumbled on the dark, narrow stairs, but used the handrails to propel himself to the top. He reached Danielle, but not before Armand threw open the door to the roof. Two steps out into the open, someone on the other side swung a two-by-four across the back of Armand's head.

Danielle screamed, then jumped out after her friend, who'd fallen to the ground, clutching the back of his skull. She'd covered Armand's body with her own, but twisted so that she could see who'd attacked them. Her eyes widened for a split second, before they narrowed into slits of rage. She knew Armand's attacker.

Despite his instinct to rush after them, Nick pulled back into the shadows of the staircase, waiting. He strongly suspected that whoever had knocked out Armand had actually been aiming for him.

"Where is it?" Danielle asked, her teeth clenched in barely checked rage.

A female voice answered. "Where it needs to be. With me. God, you don't understand! How could you? For months, I've thought I was going insane. Little pictures always popping into my head. Visions of things that never happened to me. Feelings I couldn't control. This bottle is showing me the truth. I finally understand!"

The minute Nick connected the voice to a face, the blood in his veins hardened to ice.

Margo.

BENEATH HER, Armand groaned. Danielle thought she'd never heard a more wonderful sound. Margo could have killed him! And might yet. She'd thrown her entire weight onto him, trying to keep him still and out of Margo's line of sight. She had no idea how badly Margo had hurt Armand with her first blow, but judging by the glazed wildness in her eyes right now as she shook the wood plank menacingly at them, Danielle knew he was better off on the floor. Apparently, sanity wasn't an asset Margo had in generous supply.

Danielle silently thanked Nick for having the forethought to remain in the stairwell. Margo probably thought the man she'd clobbered was Nick, not some stranger. No telling how she'd react to finding out she was wrong.

Danielle didn't want to find out. If she could calm the woman, she might find out what had caused this unprovoked attack. And then maybe, she could talk Margo out of doing any more harm.

"Margo, what are you doing? Why did you hurt him?"

The questions only enraged Margo further. She lifted the plank up higher and screamed, a mixture of agony and frustration that shot through Danielle's skin. She scrambled, covering as much of Armand's body as she could with her own. She had to trust, if just for a moment, that Margo wouldn't hurt him again if Danielle remained his shield.

"Margo, stop! He's not going to hurt you!" Danielle cried.

The heavy plank wavered above Margo's head. Her arms shook from the weight. Or from anger. Danielle wasn't sure which.

"He's not right for you, can't you see that?" Margo wailed. "He's charming to all the women, a sought-after lover, but he won't be true to you! He doesn't know the meaning of loyalty. He doesn't believe in the bonds of a man's word. He's the one who forced you to go to your father. He's the one who made you break your vow."

Danielle blinked, trying to process what the hell Margo was talking about. None of it made any sense. She'd made no promises or vows to anyone, and she'd had no contact with her father in years. Desperate, Danielle glanced toward the stairwell that led downstairs. In the shadows, she saw Nick move. He'd crouched low and his dark hair and eyes blended with the darkness.

Suddenly, an explanation occurred to her. Margo wasn't talking about Danielle—she was talking about Sofia. To Sofia. The vow she spoke of was the promise of marriage between Sofia and Milosh—the man Nick had suspected had been reborn into Armand. Could Margo—not Armand—have been the recipient of Milosh's tortured soul?

This was all supposition. For all she knew, Margo

suffered from some other delusions Danielle knew nothing about. Danielle recognized all the signs. The dizzy way Margo swayed from side to side. The watery glaze over her eyes. The shaking. Margo had all the symptoms of someone using stimulants—cocaine, maybe meth or ice. The woman Danielle had met in the coffee shop would never have as much as taken a toke of a joint, much less graduated to serious drugs, but apparently, she had.

Danielle swallowed and concentrated on not saying the wrong thing. If Margo took a swing at her, she might block the first blow, but she'd likely have two broken arms to show for it.

And more importantly, Danielle knew that if Margo struck out at her, Nick would attack. She didn't want to see Margo hurt unless absolutely necessary. She obviously wasn't in control of her own actions.

"Margo, I honestly don't know what you're talking about. Please, please explain to me. I don't want anyone else to get hurt."

Instantly, tears streamed down Margo's face. She glanced from Danielle and Armand huddled on the floor to the wooden weapon she clutched in her hands. For an instant, Danielle thought she looked surprised, as if she had no idea why she was threatening them with a plank.

"I don't know," she said softly.

Armand moaned, and managed a curse. Staying as low to the ground and close to him as she could, Danielle climbed off his body and moved so that she could examine the back of his head.

"*Ne bouge pas. Je vais t'aider,*" Danielle whispered

against his ear, promising to help him if he just remained still.

He complied, whether by choice or lack of strength, she didn't know. A huge welt had formed near the base of his skull and a gash soaked his collar with blood. Luckily, Danielle knew that head injuries could be deceptive. Skull wounds swelled quickly and bled like hell. But she wasn't a doctor. She had no idea how much damage Margo had done—or how much time they had to find out.

"Please, Margo. Put down the plank. Sit beside me. Right here." She patted the concrete. "Tell me what's going on."

Margo shook her head. "I'm not Margo, don't you see? That's it! That's why I can't think. I can't breathe." She panted, the plank lowering as she clutched at her chest. "I'm not me. But I don't know who I am. I just know I have to have you. You belong to me, Sofia. He doesn't deserve you. Should have been him at the cliff. And you know that, don't you?"

The glazed quality returned to Margo's eyes. The more she spoke in a voice that wasn't quite her own, the more strength seemed to inject into her arms.

Danielle glanced away for a moment, then gasped when a scene flew across her memory like a match struck against the side of the box.

Sofia answering the door of her *vardo,* speaking in a language Danielle had never heard. And yet, she could understand every word.

"Milosh, what are you doing here? Is Ana all right?"

The tall, blond man entered without invitation and

answered in the same foreign tongue. "Your cousin is fine. Sweet and kind and quiet. An ideal wife, only she is not you."

Danielle couldn't see Sofia, since she was in her body. But she experienced her exasperation, felt her hands fly out in front of her in a frustrated stopping gesture. "Milosh, enough! You married Ana. I married Nicholai. What's done is done. We are family now, by marriage. For this alone I don't send you away."

Milosh's face revealed nothing. Did he hear her? Did he understand? Her mouth was dry and tired from telling him the same thing over and over and over. For a brief instant, she considered finally telling Nicholai about Milosh's constant badgering about their broken engagement, but she feared the consequences. Nicholai was not a violent man, but he would do whatever was necessary to protect his family.

Accusations could divide the clan. Though Milosh was new to their family, he'd ingratiated himself to all the right people. Nicholai, who cared nothing for the opinions of others, kept to himself, satisfied with a world that included very few people beyond his immediate family. His grandmother, Jeta. His cousin, Alexis. And of course, herself. She had to handle this on her own, once and for all.

"Why are you here, Milosh?"

"I have a project to show Nicholai."

"He is not at home," she answered briskly, glad she could finally rid herself of her former suitor, if only for a few hours. Jeta and Alexis had gone to tend a sick child in the village. Nicholai had left a half hour ago on an errand. She was alone and something in Milosh's expression made her stomach clench with fear.

"A *gaujo* man sent a servant," she explained, "bidding Nicholai to repair a damaged railing at his home. He should be back by morning."

"There is no damaged railing," Milosh muttered.

"What are you talking about?"

She'd had enough. She stalked to Milosh and fisted a handful of his shirt in her hand. "Where is Nicholai? What have you done to him?"

Danielle blinked, and the memory dispersed. She glanced up at Margo just as she raised the plank higher. With one swift downward thrust, Danielle's skull could be crushed.

"Milosh, don't!" Danielle screamed.

She pulled her legs beneath her, trying to arrange her footing in case she had to rush Margo. She couldn't merely roll out of the way. If she did, Armand would take the blow meant for her, a strike that might mean permanent damage, even death. Danielle couldn't allow that to happen. She knew how to protect herself—and the ones she loved.

Like Armand. Like Nick.

Danielle knew how to fight. But Sofia had not.

The rest of the story rushed back into her brain in a series of flashes that nearly blinded her. Milosh claiming to have taken Nicholai into the woods and harmed him. Sofia begging Milosh to lead her to him. The mad dash up the mountain. The windswept desolation of the ledge. Milosh pleading with her there, pledging his love and devotion, promising to break with her cousin,

Ana, kindly if only Sofia would take her rightful place as his wife.

She'd refused.

Fool, Danielle thought now. She should have lied. Danielle could feel the placating words rolling like silk off her tongue, saying anything to get off the damned cliff.

But Sofia had possessed no such guile. Instead, she'd lamented Nicholai's absence, lamented being sent on a fool's errand by a madman crazed by betrayal and desire. No one had remained to save her from Milosh's obsession. She'd had nowhere to run when she'd spurned him, no hand hold to cling to when he'd pushed her over the cliff.

Danielle grabbed Armand on one side, the floor on the other, anything to stop the overwhelming sensation of falling. She was suddenly aware of their position on the roof. The ledge was only a few feet away. Had Milosh lured her here again to repeat his murderous intentions from the past?

She glanced into the shadows of the stairwell. Was Nick still there? Her vision, offset from sudden vertigo, wavered, unable to focus. If only Margo would put down the plank, perhaps history could change. No one had to die.

Danielle could make the difference. She took a deep breath, carefully softening her voice to a sympathetic whisper.

"You didn't mean to kill me, did you, Milosh?"

Rage widened Margo's eyes. "Don't call me that!"

"That's who is inside you," Danielle said, forcing

her tone to remain steady and calm. "That's the voice you hear, the one who makes you want me."

Margo's face softened and tears dropped from her eyes. "I don't understand. I'm not like this. I'm not. But when you said how well the construction was going, how you'd be done and out in six weeks, I couldn't bear it."

"So you sabotaged the scaffolding," Danielle guessed. Now this was starting to make sense. Beside her Armand rolled on his side and she could see that his eyes were blinking, but alert. She pressed her hand on his shoulder, willing him to stay still.

"I didn't want to hurt you," Margo said softly. "I just didn't want you to leave."

"And the fire?"

Wrong question. Fury erupted and Margo screamed. She dashed toward her, the plank ready to strike, but at the last moment, she stopped.

Tears plopped down her face like fat raindrops. "He was with you. Making love to you. All those nights I stood outside your *vardo*, listening, imagining me on top of you, driving myself into your soft warm flesh."

Margo reached out and nearly cupped Danielle's cheek when Nick appeared behind her, yanking the plank from her hand and tossing it aside. Margo spun on him, enraged. She clawed at him, kicked and spat. Danielle watched in horror as Nick tried not to hurt Margo, but instead backed up, avoiding her blows, but retreating closer and closer to the building's ledge.

Beside her, Armand groaned, louder than before. "Armand, are you all right?"

"She nearly killed me."

Danielle couldn't argue, but right now, Nick needed her help. "Don't move. The last thing I need is you blacking out."

She went to stand, but Armand grabbed her hand. "She's insane, *ma petite*. Let the pirate handle her."

Danielle tugged her hand free. Nick was a gentle man. And apparently, he hadn't been waiting in the stairwell the entire time. Since he'd come up from behind her, Danielle guessed he'd backtracked out of the building and then climbed up the fire escape. He hadn't heard Margo admit that the spirit of Milosh was driving her out of her mind, meaning he might not anticipate the sheer strength and lack of fear that Margo possessed now that the boundaries of her sanity had been stripped away. He didn't know that Margo, or at least, Milosh, craved his death.

Danielle also recognized that Margo was high as a kite, likely using drugs in a vain attempt to quiet the soul of a madman locked inside her. She was dangerous. And Danielle wasn't about to allow the spirit of a jealous gypsy to rewrite history so that Nick fell to his death instead of Sofia this time.

They'd reached the ledge. Nick had Margo's hands locked in his. He tried to twist them behind her back, but Margo side-stepped him then lashed out with her knee, connecting the hard bone with his stomach. When she went for a second blow, he jumped backward. His legs collided with the short railing around the building and his balance wavered.

Danielle rushed Margo, determined to pull her off Nick and give him time to regain his balance. She grabbed her by her waist. Using all her strength and the element of surprise, she yanked her backward, flinging her away from them. Margo stumbled, but regained her footing. With an ear-piercing cry, she lunged at them, perhaps to throw both of them over the edge. But Armand, with the reclaimed wood plank, smacked Margo across the back. She crumbled to the floor, writhing in pain.

"*Ce n'est que justice, salope,*" Armand spat.

Danielle turned. Her friend had doled out a bit of cruel justice, but only because he'd had no other choice. She took a look at Nick's face and winced at the bloody claw marks there. They were both panting, out of breath. She reached out to dab a streak of blood about to drip into his mouth, but he caught her hand. "Why did Margo attack us?"

Danielle glanced back at Armand, who stood over the thrashing Margo with fury and determination in his eyes. If the woman moved in any way he found threatening, Armand was prepared to strike again. After a moment, Margo shaped herself into a ball and began to sob.

"She's Milosh, Nick. She's been hearing voices that are not her own, making her do things like sabotage the scaffolding and set the fire. I think she even tried drugs to quiet him. I could have told her. Drugs only make the voices worse."

Nick put his arm around her.

"So she stole the bottle?"

Danielle shook her head. She didn't know if Margo had been responsible for the theft, but she felt certain she'd intentionally lured them to the roof by slamming the door in the stairwell. She'd followed instincts bred into her body for a century. She'd expected Danielle and Nick to come running, but hadn't banked on Armand.

Once certain Armand had the situation under control and Margo wouldn't attack again, Nick and Danielle searched the roof and the stairwell for the bottle, but found nothing. She didn't respond to their questions or pleas. Soon after, sirens announced the arrival of the police. After hearing a carefully modified version of the story, they carted Margo away for a psychiatric evaluation and perhaps, robbery and attempted murder charges. Danielle fought valiantly to contain her tears at Margo's ravings as the police dragged her down the stairs in handcuffs. She loved her! She would never hurt her! Only Nicholai had to die! Only Nicholai!

With a little prodding, Armand succumbed to a police officer's insistence that he submit to a check by the paramedics who'd arrived downstairs. Nick and Danielle gave their statements to the police on the roof, but refused to go down since neither of them was hurt, except for the scratches on Nick's face. Once alone, Danielle retrieved a first-aid kit from Nick's workshop and cleaned the wounds herself.

"The bottle isn't here, is it?" she asked after she had Nick settled on the roof floor. She dabbed antibiotic ointment on a cotton swab and readied the bandages.

"She might have thrown it over the edge. We can check for shards in the morning. It's too dark now."

Danielle frowned. "Your gypsy king won't be happy."

Nick grinned, wincing when she made first contact

with a particularly deep gash on his chin. "Viktor will live. The bottle had sentimental value to him, that's all."

"It was probably priceless!" she insisted.

He shrugged. "Doesn't matter, because I know he would never have sold it."

Danielle took her time with his cuts, not wanting Margo's fingernails to permanently scar Nick's face. His absolutely perfect, rugged face. A face she'd known in her heart for a hundred years at least, and one she felt certain she'd never grow tired of looking at.

"I wonder if she ever had the bottle at all. She didn't have the tools," Danielle pointed out.

Nick contemplated what she'd said, then dismissed the topic with a shake of his head. "It's a shame, really. Milosh's voice was driving her, making her feel things and do things she obviously didn't understand. She had all these memories and visions and she didn't know where they were coming from. If she'd touched the bottle, it might have given her clarity."

Danielle snorted. "The bottle might have made her experience worse. Look what the drugs did. She was self-medicating. Probably thought she was schizophrenic. The drugs explain why she was so strong and why she wouldn't back down."

"But now it's all over."

The finality in his voice spawned a tightening in her chest. She'd finished working on him, so she gathered the bloody swabs, wrapped them in gauze and shoved them into the kit.

She took a deep breath, then asked the question that could change her life forever.

"All over, or just beginning?"

Never in her life had Danielle Stone considered herself an optimist. Since her seventh birthday, she'd been inherently focused on the negative, drawn to the dark possibilities of both life and love. Armand had coaxed her from that melancholy, but until she'd met Nick and finally felt whole, looking at the positive possibilities had always been a chore.

Yet here, in the light from the street, on top of a dirty old warehouse on a muggy, summer night, she saw the future as clear as the water of Lake Michigan. Blue and bright and sparkling, if Nick only said the words.

Would he say them first, or would she? Denying now that she loved him when they'd just faced down their mortality seemed a waste of time. The love Sofia had nurtured for Nicholai still existed within Danielle and she could no more deny the power of the timeless emotion than she could deny the danger they'd faced tonight, together. Sofia had loved Nicholai for his charm and wit and passion. Danielle loved Nick for all those things, as well as his honor and courage and patience. He'd skillfully presented her with the layers of an unbelievable story, and yet, his sincerity had inspired her to believe. And even though she still suspected his soul was as old as the memories inside her, he'd adjusted to who she was now and respected her hard-won independence. He'd shown this in so many ways.

"Why didn't you rush in from the stairs?" she asked.

"Too dangerous. I heard you talking to her, knew you'd keep her from attacking long enough for me to find another way onto the roof where I could surprise her. I think she believed Armand was me when she hit him. She didn't expect a third person in the stairwell."

She nodded, knowing this made sense. "So you trusted me to handle myself."

He rolled his eyes. "With all your talk about surviving on the streets, I figured you could handle one drugged-out maniac for a few measly minutes."

Danielle laughed, but wasn't fooled by Nick's smile, which wrinkled at the corners of terrified eyes. He'd seen his soul mate in imminent danger. And yet, he'd trusted her to handle herself while he moved into a better position to assist. He'd believed in her. Her mouth dried at the same time that her eyes filled with tears.

"What's wrong? Are you hurt?" he asked, gingerly cupping her face and drawing her near.

She shook her head, unable to speak.

"Danielle, let's go inside."

With a grunt, he stood, then extended his hands, which she took eagerly. The minute he tugged on her, she felt lighter than air. Instead of just standing, she couldn't resist leaping up, so that he had to catch her to keep her from falling.

And of course, he did.

She threw her arms around his neck and kissed him with every fiber of the woman she'd been in another life, every inch of the girl who'd lived on the streets and every aspect of the lover who could easily imagine spending the rest of her life in his arms. She locked her legs around his waist, extracting a growl from deep inside his chest. He buoyed her bottom with his hands and the moment his fingers started to roam, she knew where she'd be when the sun finally rose.

In his bed, where she belonged. For now and for always.

Epilogue

"KEEP YOUR EYES CLOSED until I tell you to open them."

Nick positioned Danielle in the center of the room, then stalked to the wall and flipped the switch.

The moment he heard Danielle's delighted gasp, he grinned from ear to ear. She hadn't kept her eyes closed, as he'd ordered. Nothing new. Following rules was not her forte and at this moment, he didn't give a damn. The overjoyed expression on her face made every splinter, every gouge in his fingers, every late night working on her surprise well worth the effort.

"Oh, my God! Nick, how did you…"

Her question trailed away as she spun in the bedroom of their new condominium. She turned slowly, her eyes as bright as the tiny pinpoint lights he'd built into the hand-carved shelves. Sparkles shot at her from each of the blown glass or faceted crystal perfume bottles they'd collected over the past six months from, so far, fourteen separate countries. They'd amassed over one hundred pieces, some from cheap tourist shops, others purchased from museum-quality collections, seeking to replace the bottle that as of yet, had not been recovered. Each new phial had become a memento from a half year Nick knew he'd never forget.

With a quivering hand, she glided toward their favorite find, a ruby-red atomizer that had once belonged
to a sultan's beloved concubine. She lifted the perfume
bottle from the mirrored stand and gave the bulb a
squeeze. A scent as old and exotic and spicy as a desert
oasis floated into the air, sparking Nick's memory of
their trip to India, where they'd stayed in a medieval
palace still owned by the royal family who ruled the
area. The bottle had been a gift from the princess,
who'd heard about their burgeoning collection. That
night, he and Danielle had made love with moonlight
streaming in from the desert, the scent of the ancient
perfume floating around them on their silk bed. Tonight, they'd make love on the bed he'd created for
her, surrounded by the spoils of their travels and en-
sconced in a love Nick never imagined could feel so
new, and yet, so timeless, at the same time.

"I can't believe you did all this!" Danielle ex-
claimed, replacing the bottle before she turned and
jumped in his arms. "Thank you!"

He spun her carefully, invigorated by the adoration
in her eyes.

"See that blank wall, there, above the bed?"

She reluctantly looked away from him, grinning
shyly when she spied the beautifully stark space, already prelit with tiny lights. "Is that for me, too?"

"This is all for you. But I expect you can paint your
most private masterpiece above our bed, for only the
two of us to enjoy."

She kissed him then, long and hard and hot. The
taste of her injected him with a unique magic unlike
any ever created by his people. The flavors tripped

every sensual wire in his body, ensuring that he'd never be able to part from her. Never.

When they'd first met, he'd believed that once Danielle accepted that she was the reincarnated soul of his beloved Sofia, they would marry, have children, settle down somewhere in the center of the country, where they could fulfill his gypsy yearnings for travel on any given day. He hadn't factored in the influence of the woman she'd become in her new life.

Nothing that he'd predicted had come to pass, and in retrospect, he was glad. It hadn't been enough for him to love Sofia, the woman she'd been, and admire Danielle, the woman she'd become. To satisfy Danielle's needs, he had to love the new woman more than he loved the old. She'd insisted they take the time to see if he could love her and despite his desire to close the chapter between his two lives, he'd agreed. They promised to take one day at a time, to build on the passion borne in another lifetime. The truest test came when he'd finally disclosed the full story about his past—about his death and reanimation.

She'd retreated from him for two days—forty-eight hours that rivaled the century he'd spent in the twilight plane between the world of the living and the world of the dead. Finally, she'd returned to him, claiming that she no longer cared about how he'd come into her life, just that he was finally back where he belonged.

But when her brother had offered her a position overseeing a collection of investments he'd made around the globe, Danielle had jumped at the chance, causing Nick to fear that separation would end their affair. Then she'd begged him to come along. He was a gypsy, after all. And traveling in a private jet beat a secondhand *vardo* anytime.

Pillow Talk had opened on time, on budget and to great success. For a weekend reservation, even the rich and famous had to call four weeks in advance. And Nick's craftsmanship had spawned dozens of orders for carved beds from patrons who'd fallen in love with the ones in the restaurant. He'd been able to charge prices he would never have imagined people could afford, and had hired a staff to do the majority of the work, leaving the intricate carving for him during his infrequent trips home.

They'd attended Pillow Talk's opening night, but had spent the majority of the past six months jetting from Bangkok to London, from Sydney to Taipei. Sebastian Stone possessed an incredibly diversified portfolio and Danielle had found her niche in making sure her brother's interests in everything from oil refineries to luxury hotels were being managed with care. When she'd invited Nick to join her, his wanderlust had found an amazing means of satiation. While she tended to business, he explored. In the evenings, they shared the spoils of his meandering, including all the perfume bottles now housed in what would soon be their home.

"I want you to love everything about this room," he said with a seductive grin, well aware that Danielle had chosen the condominium mainly because it was minutes from the private airport where Sebastian kept his plane. "Every time we're here, I want you to be surrounded by memories of our new time together."

He sounded hopelessly sentimental, and he didn't care. Since he'd walked onto that construction site six months ago, they'd gone on a roller coaster ride of passion, danger and now, exploration. Only last week, he'd come to the conclusion that they'd finally put the negative events of their initial meeting to rest, after visiting Margo at the St. Lucius Psychiatric Hospital in California. Margo had been weaned off the drugs and her prognosis had been positive. She'd admitted to Danielle that flashes of someone else's life still plagued her, but her therapists had taught her how to cope and not act on the negative emotions the visions sometimes inspired. She'd also insisted that she'd entered the warehouse only after someone else had broken in. She knew nothing about the perfume bottle or its reputed magical powers.

Danielle and Nick had agreed that explaining to Margo or her doctors about Milosh and their theory of reincarnation wouldn't help anyone. In fact, they might have both been locked up in the padded room next to Margo's for the duration.

Instead, Danielle had encouraged her former friend to continue with her therapy, which Danielle had arranged, using her brother's ample resources. They'd both admitted that Milosh was no longer a part of their lives—at least, until the next go-around.

Armand, back in Paris, hadn't agreed with Danielle's decision not to press charges against Margo for the attack. He also wasn't happy that he didn't turn out to be Milosh, evil or not. The Frenchman seemed convinced that he'd been someone in Sofia's past—a brother, a cousin, her faithful dog. Determined to return to France and explore the possibilities through past-life regression, he'd healed from his injury in record time.

He'd also seduced the nurse he'd met at Chicago General and convinced her to return to Paris with him and provide private care for his head injury. Amazingly, the couple was still together after all this time, and Danielle couldn't have been happier that her former lover had found someone to hold his interest for longer than a week. Again, Nick saw her joy as a sign. She was ready, finally, to move on.

And Nick wasn't going to waste another moment. The time was right—perfect. The scene was set. Champagne fizzled in the ice bucket next to the bed. He'd purchased an entirely new set of the Divines' edible body paints, currently sitting on a silver tray in the middle of the bed. Tucked into the night table was a special gift from Cecily Divine, a strange, red leather-bound book called *Sexcapades,* which she'd made him promise not to open until he had permission from Danielle.

So why was he sweating? Why was his heart thundering against his chest so that he was certain Danielle could feel the pounding through her blouse?

"You only want me to remember our new time together, not the old? That doesn't seem possible anymore," she said, eyes twinkling. She wrapped her arms tighter around his neck and pressed her body against his. "Though our new times have been incredibly...adventurous."

Instantly, his blood heated and his cock tightened. She could arouse him with just a glance, and with her body, she could drive him insane. Was he really ready for a lifetime of physical and spiritual slavery to a woman who would rule his heart for eternity? Did he have any choice?

"And we'll keep exploring together, Danielle. For all time, if you'll continue to have me."

He put her down and in the fashion he'd seen in countless films, he dropped to his knee and took her hand in his. She stepped back, her eyes wide, but he didn't release her, even when her hand began to shake.

"Nick, what are you doing?"

He arched an eyebrow. "What does it look like I'm doing?"

"Losing your mind."

"Seems appropriate, since I've already lost my heart."

"Oh, God." She wavered, but remained standing. She drew her free hand to her mouth and her eyes glistened with moisture. The sight of his lover nearly overwhelmed with emotion brought a lump to his throat.

"Danielle, I love you. I love who you've been and I love who you are now. I've no doubt that I will be helplessly, hopelessly in love with whomever you become in the future. But believe it or not, I could love you so much more if you'd only become my wife."

With a gasp, she fell to her knees in front of him. She took his other hand. "You've been my husband, my mate, for eternity. I know that in my soul. I love you, Nick."

Their kiss was soft and gentle, not an exploration, because they knew the territory with a familiarity that spanned time, but with a loving need he doubted they'd ever truly satiate, no matter how many lifetimes they tried.

She broke away with a teasing grin. "So, where's the ring?"

Nick pressed his lips together, waylaying a knowing smile. "On the bed."

She jumped up, spinning toward him with bright, accusatory eyes when she saw the silver tray.

"That's body paint."

"Yes, it is," he confirmed, standing.

She licked her lips. "Where's my ring?"

"Inside one of the jars, I think. Hmm," he said teasingly, brushing his body against hers while he ran a finger from her belly to her breasts. Her nipples peaked beneath her blouse and his mouth instantly watered for a taste of the woman who ruled his world.

"I can't remember if I stuck it inside Blueberry Blush or Cheeky Cherry Chocolate. Or maybe it was one of the other six new flavors. I guess we'll have to use them all up until we find it."

She ripped open his shirt with one forceful tug. "Could take us all night," she said before leaning forward and swiping a wanton lick across his chest.

"Maybe, but one thing is undeniable."

She stopped nibbling on his neck long enough to ask him, "What?"

"We'll have one hell of a good time looking."

HARLEQUIN® *Blaze*™

Members of Sex & the Supper Club
cordially invite you to a sneak preview of
intimacies best shared among friends

When a gang of twentysomething women
get together, men are always on the menu!

Don't miss award-winning author

Kristin Hardy's

latest Blaze miniseries.

Coming in...

August 2004 TURN ME ON #148
October 2004 CUTTING LOOSE #156
December 2004 NOTHING BUT THE BEST #164

Advance reviews for *Turn Me On*:

"A racy, titillating, daring read…"—*WordWeaving*

"Hot, sexy and funny…Ms. Hardy has a definite winner
with *Turn Me On*."—*Romance Reviews Today*

"Kristin Hardy begins a new trilogy with a great appetizer…
this is one hot book…think *Sex and the City* meets L.A."
—*All About Romance*

Receive a FREE hardcover book from

H A R L E Q U I N   R O M A N C E®

in September!

Harlequin Romance celebrates the launch of the line's new cover design by offering you this exclusive offer valid only in September, only in Harlequin Romance.

To receive your
FREE HARDCOVER BOOK
written by bestselling author
Emilie Richards, send us four
proofs of purchase from any
September 2004 Harlequin
Romance books. Further details
and proofs of purchase can be
found in all September 2004
Harlequin Romance books.

*Must be postmarked
no later than October 31.*

**Don't forget to be one of the first
to pick up a copy of the new-look
Harlequin Romance novels in September!**

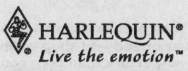

HARLEQUIN®
Live the emotion™

Visit us at www.eHarlequin.com

HRPOP0904